Devil's Reach

Clem Darby's quest for a new life brings him to New Orleans to join a Mississippi riverboat. There Clem finds a dying man, who asks him to pass a message identifying his ambushers to his gang boss, Ed Keller. But in doing so Clem invokes Keller's suspicion and becomes marked for death himself.

Meanwhile Clem learns that Keller is trying to force local girl Amy Hutton into marriage, threatening to kill her grandfather. Joining forces, they flee Keller's men and make for the Huttons' secret gold mine.

But now the word is out and their chances of reaching the mine in Devil's Reach alive become less likely by the minute.

Devil's Reach

James D. Statham

A Black Horse Western

ROBERT HALE · LONDON

ISBN-10: 0-7090-8009-3
ISBN-13: 978-0-7090-8009-1

Robert Hale Limited
Clerkenwell House
Clerkenwell Green
London EC1R 0HT

Typeset by
Derek Doyle & Associates, Shaw Heath.
Printed and bound in Great Britain by
Antony Rowe Limited, Wiltshire.

CHAPTER I

AFTERMATH OF WAR

Clem Darby had ridden the miserly trail for several days and so far there had been no hint of trouble. Somewhere up ahead lay New Orleans where he hoped to get a riverboat that would take him along the Mississippi and thence overland towards the far west.

The war between the North and the South, which had torn the country in half, had left him a grim and embittered man; sick of the long years of battle during which he had seen his comrades die in the face of cannon and musket fire. The images of entire towns and cities in flames still burned vividly in his memory.

The Confederate Army had fought well and bravely – and for what?

In the end they had lost the war and now the impoverished South was in the hands of carpetbaggers, crooked lawyers and cattle barons, determined to take over the land and build their own empires.

Now he wanted none of it. All he wished to do was push all memory of those years of war, and the subsequent time spent wandering from town to town, living by the gun, far into the back of his mind and leave it there; follow the trails of the pioneers and find himself a place far to the west where he could live in peace.

Reining his mount, he sat tall and straight in the saddle, only his rigid bearing marking him out as having ever been a soldier.

It was now mid-afternoon and the sky, which had been clear and blue for the past six days, was beginning to darken towards the east where lowering clouds threatened rain. Though he had met no one so far on this narrow trail, now all of his caution and old training came back to him.

This was something he had experienced several times in the past during the heat of battle and he knew better than to ignore it. Contraband was still brought ashore along this coastline where the river emptied into the Gulf of Mexico. As far as he was aware, slaves were no longer brought in as when the pirate Lafitte was operating in this territory, but other items were landed and there were several men in New Orleans who had grown rich from this trade.

The narrow trail in front of him spun its way down into a wide valley bordered on either side by high tree-covered hills. Slowly, he put the mount to the downward slope, letting it pick its own pace. As he rode into the valley, the rain came, a steady downpour which soon soaked through his shirt and dripped from the wide brim of his hat.

Here, in the lee of the hills, the wind from the sea eased somewhat but it still had a biting edge to it. Riding towards the crest of the hill at the far end proved to be not as easy as he had thought and as he pushed his way through the trees, he could feel the sense of unease riding with him.

His keen gaze told him that this trail, although narrow and tortuous, had been used many times and quite recently. Halfway up the hill, he dismounted, watching where he put his feet among the clumps of bitter-brush whose snaking, wiry roots spiralled from the dry soil in long, twisted tendrils.

Keeping a tight grip on the reins, he led his mount through the trees which grew more densely here than on the lower slopes. Maple and hickory grew on all sides, crowding upon the trail as if determined to prevent any passage.

At the top, he found a small, open space and squatted down on his haunches, building a cigarette and drawing the smoke deeply into his lungs. Through a narrow gap in the trees, he glimpsed a stretch of darker green in the distance and recognized he was not far from the bayou.

Tossing the cigarette butt away, he got slowly to his feet and it was then he caught the unmistakable smell of wood-smoke in the air. Tension mounted swiftly within him. It was highly unlikely he would find anyone along this trail with a friendly disposition towards strangers.

A minute later, he pinpointed the source some 200 yards away to his left. Sliding the Colt from its holster, he hefted it in his right hand, moving as silently as a shadow towards the stand of tall bushes. Beyond them, a column of grey smoke lifted into the air.

Whoever it was, they seemed to have no fear of being detected. Pushing his way through the bushes, he swung the Colt in a wide arc, his finger hard on the trigger. There was only one man there, an old man seated close to the fire.

As he stepped into view, he saw the other's hand reach swiftly towards the rifle lying close by.

'Hold it right there, friend.' Clem said harshly.

The oldster froze; then drew his hand back as he saw the gun levelled at him. After a moment, the old man said thinly, 'I ain't got anythin' worth stealin', stranger. If it's money you're after, there's some in the saddle-bag yonder. Take it: it ain't worth dyin' for.'

Clem hesitated and then holstered the Colt. 'I'm no outlaw.' he said calmly. 'I don't want your money. Reckon I'm just being cautious.'

'Guess you should be, mister, ridin' this trail.' The man squinted up at him through the slanting rain. 'I ain't seen you around these parts before.'

Confident there was no danger from this man, Clem took off his hat and shook the rain from it, then went forward a couple of paces. 'The name's Clem Darby.' he said. 'I've been ridin' this trail for nigh on six days. What might your name be?'

The old-timer grinned, showing tobacco-stained teeth. 'Colly Hutton.' He eyed Clem shrewdly from beneath bushy white brows. 'I'd say you've just come back from the war and you don't like what you see.

Now you're a bitter man with no real aim in life, ridin' a lonesome trail and lookin' for somethin' you'll probably never find.'

Clem nodded. 'I was a lieutenant with Lee,' he acknowledged, as the other motioned him towards the fire. 'I've had my bellyful of war. I just want to get well away from here, take the riverboat from New Orleans and then head west as far as I can go.'

'Well, I sure hope you find what you're searchin' for, Clem, but I wouldn't bet on it. Not in these parts, anyway.'

Hutton gestured towards the skinned deer roasting over the fire. 'Guess you'll be hungry. Help yourself. I've got plenty o' grub.'

Taking out his knife, Clem sliced off a strip of meat. It burned his fingers as he put it into his mouth, chewing slowly on it. He wondered just who this old fellow was, living out here all alone with the entire territory swarming with outlaws – possibly a hunter or prospector, not that there was likely to be any gold around these parts.

'You ain't figgerin' on riding to New Orleans through the night, are you?' Hutton enquired. He glanced up at the sorrel standing patiently nearby. 'That would be a damnfool thing to do. Reckon you're lucky to have got this far without bein' jumped by one or other o' those bands o' gunslingers from town.'

Clem studied the other with an expression of surprise. 'I ain't laid eyes on anyone all the time I've been riding. Surely there's nothin' here for anybody?'

9

Noticing his puzzlement, the other went on sharply, 'Appearances can sometimes be deceptive. New Orleans is full o' men who've got mighty rich from bringin' in contraband. There ain't many slaves brought in now, but the ships still sail in close to the gulf and bring in guns and rum which they land among the creeks from small boats.

'Most o' the important men in town are constantly at each other's throats. They've got their own men workin' for 'em. This trail is watched all o' the time and whenever a few boatloads come in, they're lucky if they ain't attacked long afore they reach town. And nobody likes strangers ridin' in that they know nothin' about, especially if they figure it might be some lawman.

'I'm no lawman.' Clem replied. 'All I aim to do is reach New Orleans.'

'That might not be as easy as you think. If you'll take the advice of an old man, you'll stay here for the night. Once you get down there,' he pointed a skinny claw towards the north, 'the Trace can be a mighty dangerous place after dark for a lone rider.'

'And you think I'd be any safer here? I spotted your fire easily enough and what could two men do against a score or more?'

The other uttered a cackling laugh. 'They won't bother with me; you can be sure o' that. Far as they're concerned, I'm just a crazy old coot who's touched in the head. I don't bother them and they leave me alone. You'll be quite safe here just so long as you stake your mount well out o' sight.'

Rummaging inside an old pack, Hutton brought

out a bottle of rye and handed it to him. Clem took several swallows before giving it back. He considered the other's suggestion and had to admit there was probably a lot of sense in what the old man said. Finally, he said, 'Thanks for the offer. I guess I'll accept it.'

'Now you're showin' some sense.'

Towards evening, the rain eased and then stopped altogether. Ragged breaks showed in the overcast and shortly after sunset, the sky cleared from the north-west. Staking the stallion inside a dense clump of trees, Clem took down his blanket and returned to the fire.

Colly was already rolled in his, having put more branches and brush onto the fire. Settling himself on the soft grass, Clem stretched himself out full length, listening to the crackle of the flames eating into the dry wood.

The heat from the fire and the eternal silence which lay over everything made him drowsy. Within minutes, he was asleep.

When he woke, it was still dark. A few feet away, Hutton lay on his back, snoring softly. Lifting his head, Clem stared around the clearing. Something had woken him but for several seconds, he couldn't figure out what it had been.

Then the sounds came again, the soft voices of men talking quietly among themselves and hoofbeats on the hard earth of the trail in the distance. Drawing his Colt, he eased his way across the grass. The moon was almost at full, throwing a net of yellow light over the trees.

Parting the bushes, taking care not to make a sound, he peered into the long shadows. In the bright wash of moonlight, he made out the trail where it wound among the trees. Shadowy figures were moving along it, men on horseback and others leading pack mules, heavily laden with boxes and canvas bags.

Scarcely daring to breathe, he lay there watching tensely as the long column passed across his line of sight. If any of the men smelled the smoke from the fire, they gave no sign. Evidently Hutton had been telling the truth when he had said these smugglers paid no attention to a crazy old man wandering around in the woods.

He waited tensely until the last man in the line had vanished down the steep slope to his right, then went back to his blanket, rolling himself into it. Around him, the night was still and quiet.

Ten minutes passed and he was just drifting back into sleep when a fresh sound shattered the silence. The staccato rattle of gunshots, distant but clearly audible, broke out. He thought he detected faint shouts coming from somewhere along the trail. The firing lasted for quite a while and then gradually diminished.

When there was no further sound, he turned over onto his side and closed his eyes. The next minute, he was asleep again.

He woke to the harsh crowing of birds, to find his companion already awake, frying bacon in an iron skillet and there were beans heating in a pan over the fire.

'You sleep all right?' Hutton queried. He gave Clem a sharp look and there was an enigmatic expression in the other's eyes.

'Woke up sometime early in the mornin'. There were men movin' along the trail yonder with pack horses. Little while after that, I picked out the sound o' gunfire further down at the other end of the valley yonder.'

Hutton evinced no surprise at this. Spooning beans onto a metal plate, he added several slices of the bacon and handed it across to Clem. 'Like I said, the Trace ain't the kinda trail for men to ride unless they know what they're doin'. Whoever you saw, they must've run into trouble on the way back to New Orleans. Ain't likely any of 'em would get through this time.'

'Ain't there any law to stop 'em?' Clem asked incredulously.

Hutton grinned. Between mouthfuls, he said, 'Sure there's some kind o' law. They have a town committee but since most o' the men on it are dealin' in this illegal trade, they make damned sure it still goes on. Lafitte did it for years and nobody made a move to stop him. That French pirate and his men used to walk the streets in daylight.

'But any strangers ridin' in are watched all the time. They either work for the big men there, or their lives ain't worth a plugged nickel. Take my word for it if you still intend goin' there.'

'I'll bear that in mind.' Clem promised. He ate ravenously, squatting beside the slowly-dying fire. Glancing up, he asked, 'What is it you do out here all

13

alone, old-timer? You must've been here for quite a while if those gunhawks know you well enough to leave you alone.'

For several moments it seemed the other did not intend to answer him. He sat staring into the fire, looking at nothing. Then he said, 'I've been here for nearly six years. Before that I was a scout for the wagon trains headin' west. Now and again, I go into New Orleans for provisions like coffee and whiskey but apart from that, I live off what I can find.'

Cleaning the empty plate on the grass, Clem built a cigarette, blowing the smoke into the air. 'You figure on doin' this for the rest o' your life?'

'Nope. There's somethin' I aim to do before I die.' He threw Clem an oblique glance. 'But that's somethin' nobody else knows about. I like you, young fella, and you're the first honest man I've met in years, but the less you know about this, the better.'

Clem did not question him further. Whatever secret the old man had, it was clearly something he did not intend to talk about. Getting to his feet, he unhitched the sorrel and threw the saddle on, tightening the cinch under the animal's belly.

'Guess I'll be ridin' out now, old-timer.' he said genially. 'Thanks for the grub and the company. Maybe we'll meet up again sometime.'

'Could be,' agreed the other. 'Just watch your back while you're in New Orleans. It might seem a fine town on the surface but it's still growin' and there are a lot of lawless men there. If I were you I'd steer clear of Ed Keller and Hector McFee.'

'Keller and McFee?'

14

'That's right. They're the biggest men in New Orleans, own most o' the town between 'em. Anyone goes against either o' them, they don't live long.'

'I'll keep their names in mind.' Turning the sorrel, he cut back across the open space towards the trail. A backward glance showed him the old man still sitting by the dying embers of the fire, staring at nothing.

Riding over a long stretch of bare rock, below the rise of a crest, the sorrel suddenly shied away from the trail. Clem reined up sharply, his eyes flicking in all directions, searching for whatever had spooked the horse.

At first, he could see nothing. Then, just inside the thick undergrowth, he made out four bodies. Dismounting swiftly, he went forward, his Colt at the ready. It was immediately obvious that no one had made any effort to conceal them. Bending, he examined them closely.

All four had been shot at close range and a quick glance told him that all of them still had their guns in their holsters. None of these men had had a chance to defend himself. So this was the explanation of the gunfire he had heard during the night. Whoever had done this must have been lying in wait for that column of men moving along the trail from the creek.

A little further on, he came across three more men. Two were dead but, as he approached the third, the man uttered a low groan and tried to lift his head. There was blood on his shirt where the slug had entered and even a cursory glance told Clem the other did not have long to live.

As he bent over him, the man lifted an arm and grasped Clem by the wrist. His throat muscles worked as he tried to get words out. 'It was McFee's men. They . . . they jumped us along the trail and got away with all the merchandise. Let . . . let Keller know, I—'

The man's head fell back and his hold on Clem's wrist loosened. There was a faint rattle in his throat and then his eyes went vacant, staring up at the branches above him, but seeing nothing.

Grimly, Clem went back to where the sorrel was waiting and swung up into the saddle. What he had just seen amply confirmed Hutton's words. Clearly, the old man knew far more of the activities of these two warring factions than those in New Orleans believed.

Touching spurs to his mount's flanks, he rode swiftly along the winding trail, feeling some of the old bitterness coming back. Even though the war was over, it seemed that the fighting and slaughter were still happening.

It was a couple of hours after midday when he sighted New Orleans. Down by the river, a paddle-boat stood near the levee. Large bales of cotton were being moved along the gangwalk and there were several people boarding the vessel. The narrow alleys which bordered the waterfront were a bustling hive of activity.

He rode slowly, past the French quarter, towards the main part of the town, giving the folk on the boardwalks only a cursory glance. Inwardly, he was wondering what to do about what the dying man had told him. He wanted no part of this feud between Keller and McFee but from what Hutton had said, men such as himself were looked upon with suspicion, even here.

He didn't doubt that while the authorities would openly frown upon these illegal contraband activities, behind the scenes they would be quite prepared to turn a blind eye to them. It undoubtedly brought money into the town, most of which would go to swell the coffers of seemingly respectable people, the prosperous owners of the plantations and cotton fields.

Halfway along the dusty street, he spotted a saloon and, dismounting, he tethered the sorrel to the rail outside. Before going in, he stood for a while on the boardwalk, casting a keen eye over the town. The recent war had acclimatized him to the wide, open spaces and the feel of all these grand buildings around him made him feel trapped.

After smoking a cigarette, he hitched the gunbelt a little higher around his waist and stepped inside. The lobby was dim with little sunlight managing to penetrate the dust-smeared windows.

There were two bartenders behind the counter and both of them gave Clem a queer look as he walked over. For an instant, he wondered if all strangers here were subject to this kind of scrutiny.

One of the men sidled along the bar in his direction. 'What'll it be, stranger?'

'Whiskey,' Clem said quietly.

Reaching under the bar, the other brought out a

bottle of rye and a glass. There had been no hint of welcome on the other's fleshy features and Clem noticed that several times, the bartender threw a swift glance beneath the counter. Obviously, there was a weapon of some kind there.

Without turning, Clem surveyed the room through the mirror behind the bar. Even at that time of the day, there were around a score of customers, a few dressed in long frock coats, but most of them were evidently gunmen. There was something about these men which puzzled him and for a moment, he couldn't figure out what it was.

Then it came to him. One group occupied five tables at the far end of the room while the others were clustered in a tight knot against the opposite wall. Without having to ask, he guessed that one bunch were McFee's men and the other lot worked for Keller.

After what he had witnessed along the Trace, he could understand the tension in the atmosphere which he had sensed the moment he had walked in. Pouring some of the whiskey into his glass, he sipped it slowly and then motioned to the bartender who had served him.

He saw the other hesitate momentarily before walking over. Leaning over the counter, Clem said in a low voice, 'You seem to be expectin' trouble, friend.'

A sudden gust of expression flashed across the man's face. He ran his tongue over lips that seemed to have gone suddenly dry.

'Don't ask too many questions, mister. That way

you may get to stay alive.'

Without giving the other a chance to move away, Clem went on softly, 'My guess is that those are Keller and McFee's men.'

'What do you know about Keller and McFee? Ain't never seen you before. If you're some kind o' lawman intent on makin' trouble, my advice is get out o' New Orleans.'

Clem smiled grimly. 'Do I look like a lawman?'

'Hell, I don't give a hoot what you look like. Better finish your drink and get out before some real trouble starts.'

'That a threat?'

'Nope. Just a friendly warnin'. We don't like these gunmen in town but men like Keller and McFee run New Orleans, they make the law here, so the rest o' the citizens just have to tolerate 'em.'

Clem raised his brows, finished his drink, and poured another. Lifting his head, he glanced into the mirror and saw that the saloon doors had opened and a well-dressed man had just come in. His frock coat was open and as he walked towards the bar, Clem glimpsed the gunbelt the other wore. Twin pearl-handled guns showed in the holsters.

The man came to stand at the bar a couple of feet from Clem. Behind the counter, the bartender moved quickly towards him.

'What's your pleasure, Mr Keller?' he asked, with a note of respect in his voice.

'The usual,' Keller said. Turning slightly, he threw a hard look in Clem's direction, his lips suddenly pressed into a hard line.

The bartender moved a little way along the bar and took down what was clearly a special bottle. He poured some of it into a glass and placed it in front of Keller, leaving the bottle beside the glass.

Resting one elbow on the counter, Clem turned to face the other. 'I've got a message for you, Mr Keller.' he said quietly.

There was suspicion in every line of the other's hard features and Clem noticed the way his eyes narrowed as he threw a sideways glance towards the men seated near the wall to his right. For a moment, he seemed off balance, lost for words.

Then he said in a harsh tone, 'I don't know you, stranger. What kind o' message have you got for me?' His right hand dropped slightly towards his waist.

'I came across a bunch o' men along the Trace this mornin'. They were all dead except for one. Before he died, he told me to tell you it was McFee's men who jumped them last night and they got away with all the merchandise.'

For a moment, there was an expression on the other's face which Clem couldn't analyse. Then he said tersely, 'You seem to know a lot, mister, for some-one who's just ridden in. What were you doin' along the Trace?'

Clem shrugged nonchalantly. 'Just makin' my way here.'

Keller swallowed the whole contents of his glass in a single gulp, then refilled it with an exaggerated slowness. 'And do you intend stayin' in New Orleans?'

Clem was suddenly aware that two of the men who

had been sitting near the wall had risen to their feet and were standing behind him. Without giving away his awareness of their presence, he said casually. 'Nope. I aim to put up for the night and then take the boat as far along the river as it goes and then ride west.'

Keller considered that for several moments, staring down at his glass. Finally, he looked up. 'I reckon you don't know the situation here, mister. We don't like lone strangers ridin' in; they tend to cause trouble. Some come to work for me and I don't ask any questions about their past or whether they're on the run from the law. So long as they do their job, I protect them.'

'And does the same go for McFee?'

There was a sudden blaze of anger in the other's deep-set eyes. It was only with an evident effort that he managed to control it. 'If you're thinkin' of throwing in with McFee, I'd advise you to forget it.'

Clem shook his head. 'I wasn't thinkin' of throwin' in with anyone. I saw enough o' killin' during the war. All I want to do is ride west, clear to the Pacific and leave all o' this behind.'

'Well now, that might not be a wise thing to do. There are a lot o' mighty dangerous trails between here and the Pacific. A lot o' men never make it.' He looked Clem up and down, noticing the guns at his waist. 'I saw you from across the street when you rode in. I reckon you're fast with those guns you carry and I'm always on the lookout for a good man.'

He hesitated momentarily, then went on, keeping his voice low, 'As you seem to know, I lost a lot o' good men last night; men I can't afford to lose. I pay good wages and you could do worse than ride for me. Think it over before you make any decision you might regret.'

'Now why should I get the idea you're threatenin' me, Mr Keller?'

Keller considered that remark, then shook his head. 'That's just a friendly warnin'. In the past, I've found that anyone who turns down a job with me, goes over to McFee. That I don't like.'

'Meanin' that if I'm not on that boat tomorrow, I could find myself in big trouble?'

Keller's lips twitched into a faint smile but there was no mirth at the back of it and the hard, crafty look remained in his narrowed eyes. He tossed down his drink before saying, 'Just keep it in mind, friend.'

'I'll think about it.' Clem turned back to the bar and picked up his glass. He knew Keller was staring hard at him, that the other did not take kindly to be spoken to in this way, and was trying to keep a tight rein on his temper. He guessed that most men who rode into New Orleans would be only too willing to tie in with the other and his offer being taken as lightly as this would really rile him.

After a few moments, Keller turned away from the bar, taking the bottle and glass with him. He gestured sharply to the two men standing nearby. Out of the corner of his eye, Clem watched him go. Sipping his drink, he turned things over in his mind. Maybe he should have expected something like this, particularly as Hutton had warned him against these two important men who ran this territory.

He knew Keller wasn't sure of him. Inwardly, the plantation owner was probably wondering if he was a lawman come to probe into things in this part of Louisiana. If he should ever get that idea fixed in his mind, his own situation could become extremely precarious. With the government in the north determined to stamp out slavery and illegal trading, it would not be long before they took firm action and men like Keller and McFee would find themselves out on a limb.

Finishing his drink, he went outside, aware that Keller's eyes were on him all of the time. He allowed the swing door to close behind him and then moved a little way along the boardwalk, debating his next move. Events were moving far too quickly for his liking. The last thing he wanted was to become embroiled in this feud between these two powerful men.

After what he had witnessed along the Trace, he doubted if many of the men working for McFee or Keller lived long. He could guess how these two bitter enemies operated, bringing in gunslingers from every town along the frontier to do their dirty work for them. It would not be long before a full-scale war erupted in this territory.

Finally, he climbed into the saddle and rode slowly along the street, looking for the livery stables. He found them five minutes later in a small side alley which ran back from the main street. There were several horses there but the small, wizened oldster found an empty stall at the very end.

'You in town for long, mister?' the groom asked,

eyeing him speculatively. 'We don't get many folk comin' here unless they're working for McKee or Keller and they normally take their mounts with 'em out to the plantations.'

'I'm just waiting to take the steamer along the river,' Clem told him. 'You reckon I could get a good price for the horse and saddle if I were to sell 'em?'

The other scratched his chin thoughtfully. 'You might get a hundred dollars for the lot,' he opined finally. 'I guess I can ask around for you.'

'Much obliged.' Clem touched the brim of his hat and made his way back along the street. There were a couple of hotels on one side and he chose one which stood head and shoulders above the buildings on either side. The sign above the door intimated that this was The Silver Dollar Hotel.

The desk clerk gave him only a cursory glance although his gaze halted momentarily on the guns at Clem's waist. He lifted his brows slightly but said nothing.

'Do you reckon you can fix me up with a room for the night?' Clem asked.

'Sure thing, mister.'

'And a bath and some food?'

The other turned the book and waited until Clem had signed it. He glanced down at the name but clearly it meant nothing to him. Taking a key from the wooden rack on the wall, he handed it to Clem. 'Go to the top o' the stairs, Mr Darby, turn left and it's the second door. The water will be ready for you in ten minutes.'

Thanking the man, Clem climbed the creaking

stairs. Two men came along the passage to his right, gave him a cursory glance, then made their way downstairs. Going into the room, he closed the door behind him, took off his gunbelt and laid it on the chair beside the bed.

Moving across to the window, he looked out on the street. The sun was lowering now, throwing long shadows across the boardwalks. There was still plenty of activity. Several carriages passed drawn by fine horses. He recalled that this land had once belonged to the French and there were still plenty of signs of their occupation from the architecture to some of the voices he had heard.

Soon, it would be an even bigger place than it was now, surrounded by the plantations and wide cotton fields. Before that happened, however, the gamblers and the lawless breed would have their day.

His thoughts were interrupted by a soft knock on the door. The proprietor stood there. Almost apologetically, he said, 'Sorry to bother you, Mr Darby, but your bath is ready. If you'll just follow me.'

He led the way downstairs to a small room at the rear. A thick curtain was hung across the middle of the room. After the man had gone, Clem undressed and lowered himself into the hot water, forcing himself to relax. After scrubbing off all the dirt from the trail, he lay back in the water for several minutes. Then he dressed and went into the lobby.

Going through the door which the proprietor indicated, he found food waiting for him on one of the tables. With one exception, the rest of the tables were empty. He ate slowly, washing the eggs, bacon and bread down with scalding hot coffee.

When he had finished, he sat back, rolling a cigarette, suddenly aware of the close scrutiny he was
receiving from the man who sat at the table some feet
away. The other was tall and thin with a dark moustache, his dark hair brushed back. Clem judged him
to be in his mid-fifties.

When the other felt Clem's gaze on him, he
pushed his plate away, got up, and walked over,
lowering himself into the chair opposite Clem.

'I don't reckon you know who I am.' he said thinly.
He took a thick cigar from his coat pocket and lit it,
laying a coolly appraising glance on Clem's face.

'Let me guess,' Clem said evenly. 'You're Hector
McFee.'

Momentary surprise and consternation flicked
across the other's bland features. Then he pulled
himself tautly upright in the chair. 'You seem to have
me at a disadvantage.'

Clem gave a grim smile. 'When a complete
stranger rides into a town run by two important men
and one of 'em takes an interest in me, I guessed it
wouldn't be long before the other showed up, trying
to find out what my reasons are for being here.'

McFee had now recovered his composure.
Drawing on the cigar, he blew a ring of smoke into
the air. 'And just what are your reasons for bein' in
New Orleans, Mr—'

'Darby. Clem Darby. As I told Keller, I'm just passing through. I intend to be on the boat tomorrow
and head west.'

McFee tapped the table with his fingers. He obviously had something on his mind and was wondering how far he could go with the man who faced him, if he said something Darby took exception too.

Finally, he stopped his incessant tapping. 'I know you've informed Keller that it was my men who shot up his boys and took that contraband. That wasn't a very wise thing to do.'

Darby shrugged. 'I merely came across a dyin' man, along with several others, who'd clearly been bushwhacked without a chance to draw their guns. Those were his last words. If that's the way you do your business, it's no concern o' mine.'

'Nevertheless, you took it upon yourself to inform Keller.' There was a distinct note of menace in the other's tone and his eyes never left Clem's face. 'Whether you agree with it or not, this smugglin' has been goin' on for years. My men have also been killed workin' that trail.'

Clem gave a shrug of his shoulders. 'I fought with the Confederate Army, Mr McFee. I saw men die in their hundreds for a cause they believed in. That was war and we all knew what we were doin', but what I saw last night was sheer slaughter.'

McFee remained silent for a full minute, staring down at the glowing tip of his cigar. Then he said smoothly, 'I understand from some o' my men who were in the saloon that you turned down Keller's offer. Would you consider workin' for me?'

Clem forced a grim smile. 'Since you're the second man who's offered me a job since I got into town barely a couple of hours ago, I somehow get the feelin' both you and Keller reckon I'm a danger to you.'

He leaned forward over the table, staring directly into the other's eyes. 'Listen, Mr McFee, I've already had my fill o' killing during the war. I don't want any more if I can help it. But I'm warnin' you, if any trouble does start while I'm here, I sure will finish it.'

There was a perceptible stiffening of the other's body from his waist to his shoulders. His lips thinned down as he said coldly, 'You're threatenin' the wrong man, mister. This town can be a mighty dangerous place after dark and it can be a long time between now and that steamboat sailin'.'

Thrusting back his chair, McFee got to his feet. He stood for a moment staring down at Darby, then turned abruptly and strode out, slamming the door behind him.

For several minutes, Clem sat where he was, smoking a second cigarette. Maybe he should have kept his mouth shut about what he had seen and heard along the Trace. Now it seemed he had stirred up a real hornet's nest with both of these men on his back. He had hoped to head west and find someplace where he could let the smell of gunsmoke finally wear off. But he now had the feeling that, for their own reasons, neither Keller nor McFee intended to let him live much longer.

It was an old story along these frontier towns. Men only got rich and powerful by being completely ruthless, taking the law into their own hands and killing anyone who got in their way. A man was either with them, or against them. If a man rode in carrying guns, there was no middle way. Human life meant little to them so long as they could hang on to what they had got.

Leaving the dining-room, he made his way up the shadowed stairs to his room. There was no one in sight yet quite suddenly he had the feeling that something was wrong. It was so strong that he halted abruptly just outside his door, listening intently. A moment later, he picked out the faint sound coming from just inside the room.

Drawing his gun, he turned the knob slowly. As he had half expected, the door was unlocked, yet he knew he had locked it earlier when he had gone down for the bath. Drawing in a deep breath, he thrust the door open and went in, moving swiftly to one side, expecting a bullet to come out of the darkness. But none came.

Swiftly, his eyes adjusted to the gloom. A dark figure moved slightly close to the window.

Levelling the gun, he pressed down on the trigger, then halted as a woman's voice said softly, 'Don't shoot. I'm not carrying a gun.'

Relaxing a little, but still cautious, he closed the door and walked forward. Now he could see her clearly. She was tall and slim with long hair falling to her shoulders. There was a frightened look on her face.

'How did you get in here?' he demanded roughly, trying to cover his surprise. 'You don't know how close you came to being shot.'

'I realize that but I have to talk to you. You're the only one who can help me.'

Thrusting the Colt back into its holster, Clem said

quietly, 'In what way can I help you? I've only just ridden into New Orleans and already I have two of the biggest men in town threatenin' to kill me.'

'I know, and believe me they will if they get the chance. They get uneasy if a stranger carrying guns rides into town and they know nothing about him.'

'Then with so many men on my back, how can I possibly help you? I—'

'I have to get as far as I can from New Orleans. Not just myself – but my grandfather.'

Clem shook his head in puzzlement. 'I don't understand.'

'I'm Amy Hutton. I believe you've already met my grandfather.'

Clem's mystification turned into surprise. The old man he had met with in the woods alongside the Trace! So this was his granddaughter.

'So that's how you know about me. But when I met him yesterday he said nothin' about a granddaughter.'

'He wouldn't. My parents had a small plantation along the river. They were burned out and killed six years ago. I'm sure it was McFee's men who did it, but there was no proof and the sheriff here did nothing. Now my grandfather trusts no one. That's why he left town and went to live out in the wilds.'

'And how did you get in here?' Clem asked.

'The proprietor here is a good friend of mine. I persuaded him to give me the spare key to your room. Ed Keller wants me to marry him. If I refuse, he's threatened to have my grandfather killed. He says Colly already knows too much about what's going on out there in the bay.'

'And I guess you don't want to marry Keller.'

Amy gave a slight shudder. 'He's the last man on earth I'd marry,' she said vehemently. 'That's why we both have to get away. The steamboat is our only chance, but even then, Keller could send a couple of his men after us and take us off the boat at gunpoint. We need someone with us who knows how to use a gun.'

'And how do you get word to your grandfather in time? The last time I saw him he was miles away along the trail near the creek. And he gave me the impression he wasn't thinkin' of leaving for some time.'

A faint smile touched her full lips. 'That's already been taken care of. I sent one of our men to bring him as quickly as possible. When he hears what Keller wants to do, he'll come. He'll be here by tomorrow morning.'

Turning, she sat down in the chair beside the window. There was a forlorn expression on her face. Looking down at her hands, she went on, 'There's no one else I can turn to. McFee and Keller run this town and everyone is afraid to go against them. I know Keller: once he's made up his mind, nothing will stop him. Will you help us?'

Clem thought it over, than made up his mind. 'I guess we're both in the same kind o' trouble. I'll do anythin' I can but from what I hear, this man Keller has a whole heap of men willin' to carry out his orders, and you can be sure you and your grandfather will be watched all the time. If Keller suspects anythin', he's likely to have someone watchin' the levee.'

'I realize that but we have no other choice.'

'Then I'd suggest you and your grandfather board the boat separately. That way you'll arouse less suspicion. First thing in the mornin' I have to go to the livery stables. Then I'll make my way down to the jetty. You know what time they're boarding?'

'Ten o'clock. Once we're on board and that boat leaves, I doubt if they'll try anything there.'

'But if Keller wants you as badly as he wants me, he may send some of his men along the river to catch up with us there.'

The girl got up. Now the look of frightened apprehension on her face had been replaced by a determined expression. 'That's a risk we'll have to take.' she replied. Pausing at the door, she said softly, 'Thank you for helping us. We'll meet you at the jetty.' Closing the door, she left.

A moment later, Clem saw her from the window, making her way across the wide street towards the opposite boardwalk. He stood there until she disappeared around the corner.

CHAPTER II

DANGEROUS PASSAGE

The next morning dawned cool and misty. There was a wind blowing off the distant sea and it lifted the dust from the street, blowing it along in gritty waves between the boardwalks. Finishing his breakfast, Clem left the hotel and walked slowly and warily to the livery stables. All the way, he allowed his keen gaze to rove over each side of the street, alert for trouble.

Several people who passed him gave him curious looks and then averted their gaze. At the stables, he found the same old man he had met the previous day. There was no sign of the sorrel.

'Anyone buy my mount?' he asked bluntly.

The other nodded. 'Fella came in late yesterday afternoon and liked the look of the horse. He only offered eighty dollars though, but since I figured you wanted it sold quickly, I took it.'

'That's fine by me.' Clem replied, taking the proffered bills. It was a little less than he had hoped for, but in the circumstances it was probably the most he would get.

It was as he stepped into the main street that he noticed the two men on the opposite boardwalk. Both were lounging nonchalantly against a couple of wooden uprights, apparently looking at nothing in particular. What drew his attention to them was the fact that he was sure they were the men who had stood close to him, in the saloon, while Keller had been offering him a job.

Giving no indication that he had seen them, Clem walked on for fifty yards and then stopped. Taking out his tobacco pouch, he slowly rolled a cigarette. At the edge of his vision, he saw that both men had moved from their original position. There was no doubt in his mind they were keeping a close watch on him.

Leaning his elbows on the hitching rail, he blew smoke into the air, watching the men closely but without giving the impression he had seen them. Since they were Keller's men, there could be two reasons they were following him.

Either Keller wanted to know whether or not he boarded the waiting paddle streamer – or somehow, the plantation owner knew that Amy Hutton had spoken to him and those men were hoping he would lead them to her if she tried to get away. Whatever the reason, he had no intention of allowing them to follow him far.

He remained where he was for several minutes. Then, flicking the cigarette butt into the street, he turned into the side street which, he recalled from riding in the previous day, would lead him into the French quarter and then down towards the waterfront. Here, there were fewer people about.

Now, his earlier training in the Confederate Army took over. Slipping into a winding, rubbish-filled alley, he ran silently along it until he came across the narrow opening leading to the back of one of the houses. Gripping the Colt in his right hand, he waited.

A few moments later, he picked out voices from the end of the alley. Evidently the two men had seen him enter it and were debating whether both should follow him, or one should move further around to cut him off. The next second, he picked out footsteps approaching and instantly judged there was only one man there. Evidently, they had decided on the latter course of action.

The man was cautious, but hurrying, clearly not knowing how far ahead of him Clem might be and not wanting him to get away. Tensing himself, Clem lifted the Colt, holding it tightly by the barrel. He didn't want to risk the sound of a shot being heard.

A shadow fell across the opening. Clem had a brief glimpse of the man, saw the other turn sharply as if suddenly aware of his danger. His gun was half lifted when the butt of Clem's Colt struck him on the side of the head, just above the ear.

The other went down without a moan and one glance told Clem he would be unconscious for some time. Swiftly, he dragged the inert body through the opening. Once the man failed to show at the other end of the alley, he knew his companion would come looking for him – and the gunman would be doubly careful.

Whether these men had orders to kill him, or simply make sure he got on board that vessel without talking to anyone, he didn't know, but if he was to board that steamer, there was little time in which to find out. Making up his mind quickly, he ran swiftly along the alley, pausing at the end and risking a quick look around.

There was no sign of the second man. The narrow street facing him looked empty; too empty for his liking. Keeping his head low, he ran for the far side of the street. Here, there were no boardwalks. The dusty, hard-trodden earth extended right up to the houses. Pressing himself hard against the wall, he scanned the area intently.

There was the feel of danger all about him and he knew that second man was somewhere close by. Then a sudden movement across the street alerted him to the man's presence. He saw the other edge out of an alley mouth, both guns in his hands.

The man saw him in almost the same instant. Swiftly, he brought up his guns, going down into a crouch. Even as he fired, Clem had thrown himself down into the dust, rolling over twice before bringing up his own Colt. Swiftly, he pressed the trigger as slugs whined viciously above his head and ricocheted off the wall at his back.

He saw the gunman sway as the slug hammered into him. Then he went down on his side, the Colts slipping from his nerveless fingers. Clem waited for a couple of seconds and then ran across, the Colt levelled on the man. There was no need for a second shot. He saw where the bullet had burned its way into the other's chest, killing him instantly.

Holstering his Colt, Clem turned and ran for the nearest street. The gunfire would have alerted everyone in the neighbourhood and he could guess what kind of law they had in this town. Very soon, Keller would have men out looking for him.

Five minutes later, he emerged onto the waterfront where the steamer was already loading. There were only a few people going on board and fewer still making their way towards the jetty. As he made his way towards the gangplank, he quickly scanned those in front of him.

There was an old woman, bent like a windblown oak, being helped on board by a clean-shaven man in his late sixties. A man and woman with two children followed them, directly in front of him.

Five other people stood awaiting their turn. None of them looked like Keller or McFee's hired men. Then, as he jerked his gaze towards his left, he saw the man lounging against a couple of large bales. The other was trying to appear inconspicuous but was clearly surveying everyone who went on board. So far, the man did not appear to have noticed him. With tension and urgency riding him, he slipped cautiously to his left, moving along the front of the double-storeyed warehouse, then darted to where the bales had been stacked. From where he stood, the man was completely hidden from sight.

Easing the Colt from its holster, he moved soundlessly around the pile of cargo. Ramming the barrel of the Colt into the man's side, he hissed, 'Don't make a move, friend, or I'll let you have it.'

He saw the other stiffen abruptly, then relax slightly. 'Whoever you are, mister, you got the wrong man,' the man said, gruffly. He kept his hands well away from his gunbelt.

'I don't think so. My guess is that either Keller or McFee told you to keep a watch on everyone boarding that boat. Now move back slowly and don't make any funny moves.'

He did as he was told. Once they were out of sight of everyone on the jetty, Clem moved back a little way. Before the man could turn, he had swung the Colt, knocking him out. Catching him as he fell, Clem lowered him to the ground.

Somehow, he doubted if there would be any more keeping an eye out for him. Thrusting the gun back into the holster, he made his way quickly to where the steamboat was getting ready to leave. Running up the gangway, he went on board.

Here, he made his way into the saloon and found a seat close to the door. Already, there was a poker game in session around one of the tables. Several men were standing at the bar and he scrutinized all of them closely, knowing that any one of them could be working for either Keller or McFee. There was, however, no sign of Amy Hutton and her grandfather.

Had they managed to make it? he wondered tensely. The girl had sounded scared when he had last seen her and he didn't doubt that Keller had eyes everywhere in New Orleans. And there were so many things which could have gone wrong with her plan. In the near distance, he heard the rattle as the gangplank was hauled on board and a few seconds later, the churning of the paddle told him they were moving away from the levee.

He threw a second, searching glance around the saloon, looking for the girl and her grandfather. There was no one there matching their description. If something had happened to them, there was nothing he could do about it now. Getting to his feet, he went out onto the deck.

New Orleans was already slipping away into the distance behind them. The steamer was well into mid-river, the churning paddles thrusting it slowly upstream. Soon, they would be in open country. Going to the rail, he rested his elbows on it, watching the muddy water glide past.

Turning his attention away from the river, he ran his gaze over the few passengers on the deck. Most of the people who travelled on these big vessels were gamblers and business men who preferred to take this mode of transport rather than the overland stagecoaches. Not only were the latter slower and more uncomfortable, but there was always the risk of being held up by the outlaws who still roamed this part of the country.

He turned and was on the point of going back into the saloon when he saw the old couple he had noticed earlier coming on board. Then, he had given them only a cursory glance but now he looked more closely, aware that they were both staring in his direction.

Then the woman lifted her head and straightened up. Slowly, she drew the black shawl away from her face. Stunned, he could only stare as they walked towards him.

'Amy! I thought you hadn't made it.'

She gave him a quick smile. 'My grandfather thought it best we disguised ourselves as best we could. It was fortunate we did; there were men watching the boat.'

Clem nodded. 'A couple of them came after me into the French quarter. I had to kill one o' them. They were Keller's men, no doubt about that.'

He noticed the anxious expression on the old man's face. 'Then you can be sure Keller won't let it rest there, son. If there aren't more of his men here, they'll be waiting for you further along the river – and for Amy. I know that man of old. If he wants her for his wife, nothin' is goin' to stop him.'

Hoping to reassure the girl, Clem said tautly, 'There's a big country out to the west and I covered a lot of it with the army. Once we leave the river, there are places I've been where Keller and his men will never find us.'

'I only hope you're right,' Colly said dubiously. 'He's got a lot o' men to back him if he makes his play. These are dangerous men, Clem. Shootin' a man in the back means nothin' to them. They're pure evil – and Ed Keller is the worst of 'em all.'

'I'm beginnin' to find that out for myself. But right now, we have to make certain that none o' Keller or McFee's are on this boat.' He threw a searching glance along the deck. 'You'd better stay here. I'll take a good look around.'

'Be careful,' Amy said softly. 'Not all of the men working for Keller are dressed like you. There are business men in New Orleans who owe him many favours. Any one of those men in the saloon could be in his pay.'

'I'll keep my eyes open,' he promised.

What the girl had said was a problem which hadn't occurred to him. He had been focusing all of his attention on gunslingers, men who were easily picked out. Going into the saloon, he moved over to the bar. Apart from its smaller size, there was little to distinguish it from any of the saloons in the towns he had ridden through. Two of the tables were now occupied by poker players and, without giving any outward sign, he scrutinized the men there from beneath lowered lids.

Several of them, he guessed, were professional gamblers, working the riverboats that plied the river, men who made a lucrative living from unsuspecting players. Every one of them would have derringer hidden beneath their frock coats, ready to shoot down any man foolish enough to accuse them of cheating.

The bartender wore a spotless white apron. Evidently, those who owned these riverboats employed a higher class of person than those in the towns.

'What will it be, mister?' the man asked. His brows were lifted a little but apart from that, he gave no other sign that he had noticed the guns at Clem's waist.

41

'Whiskey,' Clem said, and waited while the other poured some into a glass.

'You travellin' far up river?' There was only one other man standing at the counter and the bartender seemed inclined to engage in conversation.

'As far as you go,' Clem replied. He turned casually and looked around the room. 'I guess these are all your usual passengers.'

'Most of 'em,' agreed the other. 'As you'll see for yourself, there aren't many on this trip. We get more on the return journey, heading into New Orleans.'

Motioning to his glass, Clem waited until the man had refilled it, then said quietly, 'I was supposed to meet one of Ed Keller's men on the boat but I don't see any sign of him. Could be he didn't make it.'

'It wouldn't be Reuben Callender, would it?'

Nodding, Clem said, 'That's right.'

'He was in here a few minutes ago. You must've just missed him. Maybe he's stepped out on deck.'

'Thanks.' Clem finished his drink and dropped a couple of coins onto the counter, moving quickly to the door.

Pausing with his hand on the handle, he looked through the glass. The deck was deserted except for Amy and her grandfather and a short, stout man dressed like a banker or store-owner. Clem instantly noticed that Callender had his right hand in the pocket of his coat. There would be a gun there, undoubtedly pointed at Colly. Amy would have to be taken alive, unharmed, to Keller and Clem felt sure Callender would expect no trouble from her.

Behind them, just beyond the stem, the large

paddles turned in their endless revolutions, churning up the water. This was going to be tricky. The noise of the paddles would certainly deaden any sound he made, but if either Amy or her grandfather should flick a glance in his direction, it would instantly alert Callender.

Then another thought struck him. It was one of the oldest tricks in the book, but it might work. Swiftly, he built himself a cigarette and thrust it between his lips. Leaving his gun in its holster, he lurched along the deck, swaying precariously from side to side, his head low.

From beneath the brim of his hat, he saw Callender turn sharply at the waist. He still kept his hand on the gun in his pocket. Feigning a drunken stagger, Clem shambled forward until he was within a foot of them.

Slurring his words, he muttered, 'Any o' you folk got a match?'

'Reckon you'll get one in the saloon,' Callender said thinly. 'You've obviously drunk too much already. Now move, friend, you're interrupting a private conversation.'

'Sorry.' Clem made to turn away. The next instant, his right hand lashed out like a striking rattler. Grasping the man's arm, he spun him round before Callender was aware what was happening.

Before Callender could use the concealed gun or regain his balance, Clem's left fist caught him full on the chin, hurling him back against the railing. He hung there for a split second and then he was gone. Clem had a brief glimpse of his body dropping between the stem and the paddles before it was dragged under the water.

Amy uttered a low cry and thrust herself away from the rail, covering her face with her hands. Even Colly's tanned features seemed a shade whiter as he said, 'Glad you showed up when you did, son. He was threatenin' to shoot me and then take Amy back with him. Guess he didn't reckon on you bein' on board.'

'How did you know?' Amy asked in a low voice.

'Better thank the bartender back there.' Clem said. 'He put me wise to him.'

'You reckon there might be any more?' Colly asked.

Clem shook his head. 'I doubt it. There were men watching the jetty when we left. Just in case they missed you, he put that *hombre* Callender on the passenger list. Reckon we're safe enough until we reach the next stop.'

It was an hour before nightfall when they came within sight of the small town which straddled the river. After checking what time the boat left the following morning, Clem went back to the others. Waiting on deck while the vessel docked, he scanned the dim length of the waterfront.

A huddle of tall warehouses lined it and there were the usual bales and boxes of merchandise standing beside them. Plenty of places where men could conceal themselves, he thought tensely.

'You think there might be trouble waitin' for us here?' Colly asked, moving up to stand beside him.

'Maybe I'm bein' over-cautious,' Clem replied. 'It

44

all depends on what Keller is thinkin' right now. Those men back in New Orleans may have told him there was no sign of you getting on the steamer and he's relyin' on Callender to make certain. If so, we may be lucky and it'll be tomorrow before he finds out for sure.'

Colly gave a grim smile. 'If so, we'll be back on that boat by the time any of his men can get here.'

Nodding, Clem led the way down onto the jetty. Several men were busily shifting bales with just one man overseeing them. Already, the other passengers were drifting towards the centre of the town. For some, he guessed, this was their destination. Others were undoubtedly heading for the hotels, rejoining the boat the next day.

By the time they reached the end of the main street, it was already getting dark. Lights showed in the various saloons, spilling out onto the boardwalks in long yellow swathes. Three hotels stood almost adjacent to each other, separated only by narrow alleys which ran back from the street into anonymous darkness.

They chose the one in the centre. Clem paced slowly towards the desk, taking in every little detail. An elderly couple stood there and he recognized them from the boat. Waiting until they moved away, he went up to the clerk, saw the sudden hardening of the man's face as his glance fell on the gunbelt at Clem's waist.

'You got three rooms for the night?' Clem asked, ignoring the expression on the clerk's features.

'Three rooms?' The man swung his glance to Amy

and her grandfather.

'That's right,' Colly said harshly.

'Of course.' The clerk's Adam's apple bobbed up and down as he swallowed nervously. 'I just thought—' He checked himself quickly and turned, taking down three keys from the rack. 'Top o' the stairs to your right.'

As they moved away, he called, 'Supper will be ready in half an hour – through there in the dining-room.' He pointed towards the door near the bottom of the stairs.

'Thanks,' Clem replied, as he followed his companions up the creaking stairs. He knew that the clerk's eyes were following him all the way, trying to figure him out.

The rooms were small and virtually identical, reasonably furnished. Going into his, Clem walked to the window and stared out. Across the street were a couple saloons, already filling up with customers. Watching them closely, he noticed that virtually all of the men going in were ordinary citizens.

He told himself that this was not cattle country and there would be very few dressed like himself and openly wearing guns. That, he guessed, explained the odd look he had received from the clerk downstairs.

A moment later, Amy and her grandfather came in. Colly closed the door behind him and there was a serious expression on his face which Clem had never seen before. Clearly, the old man had something on his mind.

Seating herself in the chair, Amy hesitated, then

said softly, 'My grandfather has something to tell you, Clem.'

Moving away from the window, Clem said, 'Go ahead, I'm listening.'

For a moment, the old man stared down at his hands, then glanced up. 'You've done a lot for Amy and me, Clem. When we first met along the Trace, I said you were probably the first honest man I'd ever met. I ain't changed my opinion since then.'

Thrusting his hand into his inside pocket, he brought out a tattered piece of paper. 'I reckon you've seen a lot of this country when you were in the war.'

Clem nodded, wondering what was coming next. 'I saw plenty.' he conceded, 'but what has that got to do with—'

'You ever hear of a place called Devil's Reach?'

Clem searched his memory, mentally listing all of the regions he had visited, then gave a nod. 'I've heard of it but, hell, it's more'n three hundred miles north o' here, out in the middle o' the most hostile country I've ever seen. You ain't aimin' to go there, are you? It's nothin' but barren hills and mountains.'

Colly leaned back, throwing an oblique glance in his granddaughter's direction. 'That night you spent at my camp, I told you there was somethin' I aimed to do before I died. I figured then you were a good man when you didn't push me to tell you what it was.'

'I figured that was your business and nothin' to do with me.'

Getting to his feet, Colly handed the paper to Clem. 'There's gold up there in Devil's Reach, more than you ever dreamed off. What you're holdin' now are the deeds to that mine.'

Unfolding the paper, Clem stared at it in stunned surprise. He knew little about these things but he didn't doubt the deeds were genuine.

Finally, he said, 'Then if these are genuine, why didn't you mine it?'

Colly twisted his lips into a grimace. 'My partner and I made that strike the last time we were returning from California after actin' as scouts to one of those wagon trains headin' west. We intended to work it but Slim caught the fever and died. I buried him out there in the hills.

'There was no way I could work that mine myself, so I decided to head back here and wait until I found the right man to be my partner.'

'And you want me to help you?'

'I've waited for nigh on seven years and I ain't met a better man.'

'I guess you've thought over the dangers and difficulties o' getting' there,' Clem said, after several moments of deliberation. 'There's a lot o' bad country to cross and even if you get there, Devil's Reach is about the worst country you could find.'

He paused as another thought struck him. His glance shifted to the girl. 'What do you intend doin' with Amy? That certainly ain't no trip for a woman.'

Before Colly could answer, Amy spoke up. 'Don't worry about me, Mr Darby. I'm not unused to hardships and I can ride a horse as well as a man.'

Clem stared at her in sudden surprise. Somehow, he had pictured her as a city woman. 'I'm not just talkin' about natural dangers, though God knows there are plenty o' them. But if anybody should get to know, or even suspect, what your grandfather has, they won't hesitate to kill him to get their hands on these deeds.'

He turned to the old man, handing the paper back. 'You sure no one knows about these?'

'I ain't ever mentioned 'em until tonight. If anyone does know, why ain't they tried to get 'em before now? They'd have had plenty o' chances while I was out there alone in the woods.'

Clem chewed that over for a moment. What Colly said was undeniably true, but he still felt apprehensive. A lot of men had been killed because of these gold strikes made in the hills to the north. He could foresee nothing but big trouble if he decided to throw in his lot with Hutton and the idea of taking the girl with them made him even more uneasy.

There was also Keller and McFee to consider. If the latter received news that he had taken the steamer out of New Orleans he might be prepared to overlook his injured pride, but Keller was a different matter. From what he had seen of him, Keller was a very determined man and he might be prepared to send men after them clear to the Texas border and beyond.

'All right,' he agreed finally. 'I'll join you, but it's goin' to be rough, particularly on you, Amy. I'd sure feel a lot easier in my mind if you were to stay here.'

The girl shook her head vehemently. 'Stay in this town and wait for Keller and his men to come looking for me? I'm going with you, no matter what lies ahead.'

Colly shrugged his shoulders resignedly. 'Ain't no point in arguin' with her. She's as stubborn as a mule once she sets her mind on somethin'.'

Clem's brows went up a fraction but he only said, 'Let's get somethin' to eat. I'm famished.'

Going back to his room an hour later, Clem locked the door, then lay on the low bed, his hands clasped behind his neck, staring at the ceiling. In the light of this new information he'd got from Colly, he tried to think things out calmly and coherently.

That brief meeting with the old man along the Trace had now led him along paths he had never wanted to travel. His original purpose of simply riding out to the California border and leading a peaceful life in that new state, had been turned completely upside-down.

In many ways, he wished he had never met up with Colly. Far from being simple, his future had now become both complicated and dangerous. He had unwittingly made enemies of the two most powerful men in New Orleans. Now he was heading north across some of the worst territory in the country.

Lying there, he gave his thoughts a protracted study, rejecting most of them without hesitation. He had given his word to ride with the old man and his granddaughter and he did not intend to go back on it. One other thought occurred to him as he lay there.

That strike had been made more than seven years earlier. A lot might have happened in that time. Prospectors were moving into that territory all the time and Colly might well find that his mine had been taken over by others, men who cared nothing about deeds and would fight to keep their hands on whatever they had found.

Taking off his boots, he placed the Colt on the small table beside the bed, lay back and closed his eyes. The hotel was quiet but in the street outside, there was still plenty of noise. The saloons were still open for business.

From somewhere, there came the sound of a tinny piano and a woman's voice singing out of tune. Several riders went by. In spite of the lateness of the hour, more men were evidently drifting into town.

When he woke it was grey dawn. Clouds had gathered during the night and there was a steady drizzle falling. It kept the dust down and there were, as yet, few people about. The rain had increased by the time they boarded the paddle steamer. This time the boat was almost empty with only six other passengers in the saloon. Clem cast an appraising glance over them, recognizing most as men who had travelled with them the previous day.

Moving towards the bar, he heard an anonymous call from behind him. 'Either of you gents like a friendly game o' poker?'

Turning, he saw the three men seated at the table near the door. Shaking his head, he rested his elbow on the counter with Amy moving towards a seat against the wall.

'What about you, old-timer?' said another man. 'You seem like a man favoured by Lady Luck. Care to have a few hands – usual stakes?'

Colly hesitated and then, before he could stop him, or warn him that these men were professional gamblers waiting to fleece anyone foolish enough to sit in with them, Colly walked over and seated himself in the empty chair.

'Stupid old fool,' Clem said, lowering himself into the chair beside the girl. 'Doesn't he know any better than to play with those crooked gamblers?'

'You can't stop him,' she replied. 'He does exactly as he pleases.'

'Then I'd better keep an eye on him, or he could find himself in trouble.'

At the table, one of the men began dealing the cards. Glancing across at Hutton, he asked genially, 'What's your name, old-timer?'

'Colly Hutton,' he replied. Picking up his cards, he failed to notice the look which passed among the three men but to Clem, watching closely, it did not pass unnoticed.

It was immediately obvious to him that Colly's name was, somehow, known to these three card-sharps. Motioning to Amy to remain where she was, Clem got slowly to his feet and moved back to the bar. He figured that none of these men was working for Keller or McFee.

They spent most of their lives working the river and they were all so adept at sleight of hand that most of their victims never realized they had been cheated. Any who did and called them out would pay for it with their lives, shot down before they could make a move.

Now his suspicions began to mount rapidly. This

52

was all part of a well-laid plan. These men weren't just out for the old man's money. There was something more behind it and his mind instantly jumped to the only possible conclusion: his name had been known to them as soon as he had given it.

That could only mean one thing. In spite of Colly's belief, these crooks knew about the deeds he carried. How they had gained this information was something he couldn't figure, but it was the only thing that made sense.

To anyone watching it would seem that Clem was taking no interest in the poker game but from where he stood, it was possible to see everything that went on. After the first three hands there was quite a pile of bills in front of Colly.

This was the usual trick these men played, allowing their victim to win several hands until they were completely hooked. Then, once they had reeled him in like a fish at the end of a line, the losing streak would begin.

'You seem to have the luck of the devil, friend,' commented one of the men, a tall, long-faced individual with a black moustache above a thin-lipped mouth.

'Guess you're right,' Colly grinned. He tossed down the whiskey which had been placed in front of him in a single gulp.

'With luck like that, I figure we should raise the stakes a little.'

Colly gave a nod. 'That's fine by me.'

One of the other men signalled to the bartender to bring more drinks for them. When he took them over, Clem noticed that two were put down for Colly and the three men barely touched theirs.

Now things were beginning to come together. No doubt the bartender was in on this deal, taking his cut from whatever these gamblers won. Perhaps there was a shotgun behind the counter, ready in the event that anything went wrong.

Around the table, two of the men had dropped out, leaving only Colly and the tall man in the game. All of the bills which had been in front of the old man were now in the middle of the table.

Taking out a cigar from a gold case, the gambler lit it and blew a cloud of smoke into the air. There was a hard expression in his close-set eyes as he tossed a further wad of money onto the table. 'I figure you're bluffin', my friend,' he said thinly. 'But I'll raise you two thousand dollars.'

At the edge of his vision, Clem saw Amy rise from her seat but with a quick, warning glance, he motioned her back.

Tautly, Colly said, 'You know that's all the money I have.'

'Then if you can't afford to see what I'm holdin', you'll lose the lot. Unless,' he added smoothly, 'you've got somethin' to cover that amount.'

'I ain't got anythin'.'

'You sure?' The man's tone was suddenly insistent.

'O' course, I'm sure.'

'Then that's mighty unfortunate, Mr Hutton. Somehow, we figured you might have a certain piece o' paper which would more than cover my two thousand dollars. After all, I could be bluffin' and with the luck you've been havin', you could win quite a tidy sum.'

'Come now, Mr Hutton.' put in one of the other men. 'As soon as you mentioned your name, we knew who you are. Those deeds might be worthless after all these years – and you sure can't work that mine by yourself, even if you reach it alive. It's more than three hundred miles to Devil's Reach and a lot can happen on the way.'

'How come you know about the deeds?' Colly muttered harshly. 'I ain't told anyone about 'em.'

The tall man smiled. 'Word like that has a habit o' getting around. Maybe you didn't talk, but your partner let it slip before he died. Trouble was you'd disappeared before we could offer to go into partnership with you. Then we heard you'd headed for New Orleans.'

'But even there you'd vanished, though we figured that someday you might go back to work your claim,' said the man on Colly's left, 'So we reckoned you'd play it safe and go by river rather than trust hitchin' up with a wagon train. Now it seems our waitin' has paid off.'

With a savage movement, Colly thrust back his chair. 'Why you damned, thieving, cheatin'—'

Before he could take a step back, there was a derringer in the tall man's hand pointing directly at Colly. 'You accusin' me o' cheating at cards?' he said coldly. 'Reckon we don't take too kindly to that and—'

Clem pushed himself a little way from the counter, only vaguely aware of Amy's sudden cry of alarm.

'Drop that gun, mister, or your crooked friends will take you off this boat feet first.'

The other stiffened, then whirled, a faint smirk on his hard features as he saw that Clem's gun was still in its holster. 'Stay out o' this.' he grated, 'or—' Without warning, he swung the derringer to cover Clem, his finger tightening on the trigger.

Clem's hand moved in a blur of speed, the Colt leaping into his hand. The single shot was deafening inside the saloon. With a howl of agony, the gambler dropped the derringer, clasping his shattered hand.

'The rest o' you keep your hands where I can see 'em,' Clem said harshly. 'And that goes for you, bartender. Reach for that scattergun you've got stashed there and it'll be the last move you ever make.'

Motioning to Colly, he said sharply, 'Just take whatever money you won. Leave 'em the rest. Then get that shotgun from behind the counter and toss it over the side.'

When the old man came back, he gestured to the two men still sitting at the table. 'Take their guns, too, and that one on the floor and do likewise.'

'You'll regret this day's work, mister,' snarled the tall man viciously. 'Even if I have to follow you clear across the country. Nobody does this to Flint Edmonton and gets away with it.'

Clem gave a brief smile. 'The next time we meet, I won't be aimin' for your hand, friend. Now I suggest you just sit there until we reach the next disembarking stage.'

CHAPTER III

DANGER SIGNALS

The journey up-river to the next stopping point took several hours. All afternoon, the dismal rain had continued with the lowering clouds promising little end to it. Darkness had fallen when they disembarked. The three gamblers remained on board but Clem knew they would not remain there long.

Edmonton would have to find a doctor soon to tend to his smashed hand and, somehow, Clem knew they had not seen the last of them. Now those crooks knew about the deeds to Colly's mine, nothing would stop them from getting their hands on that piece of paper.

Peering into the rain-soaked darkness, Clem studied the layout of the town. He didn't like what he saw. It was far smaller than that where they had spent the previous night. To his keen gaze it looked like a town which hadn't grown much since its inception, nor did it give the impression it would grow any further.

On one side of the muddy street stood a row of shanties, tumbledown buildings evidently the homes of those who worked in the nearby cotton fields. On the western side, the buildings were only slightly grander, a handful of stores, a single saloon and a cluster of old, colonial-style buildings further back from the street.

'That looks like the only hotel yonder.' Colly pointed to the single two-storey building facing the street.

He began to make his way towards it, then halted as Clem called him back. 'Somehow, I don't reckon it would be wise to put up there for the night,' he said softly.

The old man looked up at him in surprise. 'Hell, why not? It's the only place there is.'

'That's why it ain't safe. Once that crook Edmonton gets his hand fixed, they'll come after us and that's the first place they'll look.'

'Then what can we do?' Amy asked.

Clem made to reply, then grabbed the girl and Colly by the arms as he caught the sound of hoof-beats in the distance. Quickly, he thrust them across the street into the shadows between two of the shanties. The sound of the oncoming horses was loud and heavy in the mud and he recognized that the riders were heading into town from the north, not from the direction of the river.

'What is it?' Colly queried. 'You reckon it could be—'

'Judgin' by the sound o' those horses, I'd say those riders have ridden a long way – and fast.'

'Keller's men?' The old man's question was a soft hiss.

'Could be. There's no sense in takin' chances.' Cautiously, Clem edged forward and stared along the empty street. The six riders appeared a moment later, anonymous men silhouetted against the few shafts of light that spilled into the street from the saloon.

As they thundered past, he heard Colly sudden sharp intake of breath.

'I recognize 'em,' he muttered quietly. 'Those are men who ride for Keller along the Trace. You were right, Clem. Keller must have been told what happened.'

'I might have guessed they'd catch up with us sometime,' Clem said bitterly. He stared along the street to where the men slid from their saddles, still on the run. All six looped their reins over the rail outside the small building at the river end of the street, thrust open the door, and went inside.

Pulling himself back into the shadows, he remarked, 'They're obviously goin' to check with the law.'

'Surely the sheriff won't help them find us, will he?' Amy queried.

'Don't bet on it,' her grandfather replied bitterly. 'I reckon that even here Keller has some influence. He'll have figured out some trumped-up crime to charge us with.'

A sudden soft sound behind them brought Clem whirling round, the Colt jumping into his hand.

'Don't shoot, mistuh.' The low voice came from the darkness a few feet away. 'Ah couldn't help hearin' what you was sayin'. If you want to escape those men who just rode in, follow me.'

Tightening his lips, Clem stepped forward, the Colt still levelled on the shadowy shape. To his surprise, he saw it was a Negro standing there.

'What are you doin' wandering around the town at this hour?' he demanded roughly. 'And just what did you hear?'

'Enough to know that those men are after yuh for somethin'. As for bein' here, it's my job to keep a check on the cotton stores back there. It ain't any o' my business, but I figger you might need a place to hide.'

'And you know of one?' Roughness and suspicion edged Clem's voice.

'Reckon I might.'

'So why should you want to help us?' Colly asked, still suspicious.

'I've seen what those men do. I heard yuh mention a man named Keller. Even this far up the river we know of him. If those who work for him in the fields don't do their job fast enough, he whips 'em until they bleed. Now hurry! That sheriff won't wait long afore he has his men out lookin' for yuh.'

Clem knew they were taking a big risk but the man seemed genuine enough. Holstering his gun, he followed him out of the narrow opening. Beyond the shanties stood a row of wooden buildings; several dim shapes in the darkness.

Pausing in front of one of them, the man dug into the pocket of his overalls and brought out a large key. Glancing down, Clem saw there was a big lock on the door. For an instant, a stab of apprehension went through him.

'This is where we keep the cotton until it's shipped along the river,' their guide explained. 'You'll be safe here until the mornin' but it'll mean sleeping rough. Sorry I ain't got any food but we get little enough.'

Inside the building it was too dark to see anything clearly. Clem went forward cautiously, alert for any sign of a trap. Slowly, his vision adjusted and he picked out the large bales stacked across the floor.

Against one wall was a huge pile of freshly harvested cotton. 'Yuh can use that to bed down on. It'll be mighty soft compared with the floor.'

Clem glanced across at Amy, wondering what thoughts were going through her mind at that moment. It was unlikely she had ever anticipated anything like this when she had fled New Orleans.

Forcing a faint smile, she said, 'I'm so tired I could sleep on the floor.'

Clem turned to the man. 'Guess we owe you a lot. But those men are sure to search everywhere unless they figure we're out in the open country some-where.'

The other was silent for several moments. Then he said, 'There's only one way to be sure they don't find you. I got to lock you in until mornin'.' His white teeth showed in a grin. 'This ain't no trick, but that's the only way to be certain. Once they see a lock on the door, they'll figure there ain't any way you could get inside.'

Clem felt himself tighten at the other's words. The old fellow looked harmless enough, but that was nothing to go by. If any of Keller's men mentioned word of a reward for their capture, money might talk.

It seemed too big a risk to take, yet there was a note of sincerity in the man's tone, clearly noticeable.

'All right,' he said finally. 'But if this is some kind o' trap on your part, you'll be dead before those men take us. You got that?'

'I got that, mister.' There was no hesitation in his reply. After a moment, when Clem said nothing more, he turned and went out, closing the door and leaving them in total darkness. There came the sound of a key being turned in the lock – and then silence.

Striking a sulphur match, Clem held it up, lighting the faces of his companions. Both bore worried expressions. 'Guess we'd better do what he said. I'll keep watch for a while, just in case he hightails it to the sheriff's office.'

Spreading out the large mass of cotton on the floor, working only by the light of Clem's matches, they stretched themselves out on it. Before settling himself down, Clem fumbled his way to the door and stood there for a full five minutes listening intently.

There were noises in the distance, occasional nameless voices shouting to each other along the length of the street, but none of them came any closer. Then he picked out the unmistakable sound of riders heading towards the northern end of the town.

It was unlikely Keller's men would be leaving town. A more probable explanation was that they had figured their quarry had somehow slipped around them and headed into open country and could be hiding somewhere in the fields which bordered the place.

Satisfied there was little danger at the moment, he went back to where Amy and her grandfather lay. Both seemed to be asleep, but, as he lowered himself to the floor, Colly said softly, 'What do you figure on doin' now, Clem? We've got to get out o' this town – and fast and if those riders are watchin' all the trails, it ain't going to be easy.'

'I've been in tighter spots than this in the army,' Clem replied, trying to force reassurance into his tone. 'I'll think of somethin'.'

'I hope so, because right now, I'm plumb out of ideas.'

Flint Edmonton pushed open the door of the sheriff's office with the flat of his good hand and went in with Jim Dawson and Carl Winton immediately behind him. In spite of the silk handkerchief wrapped tightly around his fingers, the wound was still bleeding.

Sheriff Finlayson glanced up in surprise, then allowed his glance to stop at the other's hand. He motioned Edmonton to the chair in front of his desk.

'Somebody shot you, mister?' he asked.

'That's right, Sheriff.' Edmonton gave a terse nod.

Finlayson gave the shattered hand a closer look, noticed that blood was still dripping onto the floor. 'Don't you think you'd better get the doc to have a look at that hand, Mr—'

'Damn my hand!' Edmonton roared. 'And if you have to know, the name's Edmonton. I want the man found and brought to justice.'

'Where did this happen?' Finlayson walked around

the side of the desk and perched himself on the edge, looking down. He knew instinctively what sort of men these were – crooked gamblers trying to give the impression of wealthy businessmen as they worked the river, looking for unsuspecting victims.

'We were havin' a game o' poker with one o' the other passengers,' Dawson butted in. 'Then this old man accused my friend o' cheatin'.'

'So you drew a gun on him.' The sheriff stared hard at Edmonton as he spoke. 'And you're tellin' me this old man beat you to the draw.'

'Not him.' Edmonton spoke through tightly clenched teeth. 'This gunslinger standin' against the bar butted in. If you want my opinion, the three of 'em were in it together.'

'Three?' Finlayson's brows went up in surprise.

'There was a woman with 'em. They got off the boat and came into town together not more than twenty minutes ago. Maybe they've put up at the hotel for the night.'

'We only have one hotel in town. If they have put up there, it won't be too difficult to bring 'em in and question all three.'

Edmonton's brows drew together into a tight line across his narrowed eyes. 'I hope you ain't going to take their word against mine, Sheriff. I've got some powerful friends back in New Orleans and—'

He broke off suddenly at the sound of riders approaching swiftly along the street. The next moment, the door swung open and six riders burst in. Rising swiftly from his desk, Finlayson moved behind it as the men pushed their way forward.

'You the law in this town?' the tall, hard-featured man in the frock coat demanded roughly.

'That's right.' Finlayson ran his glance along the men, not liking what he saw. It was immediately obvious the other five riders were hired gunmen, clearly looking for trouble. 'Just what have you men got on your minds?'

'I'm Ed Keller. Could be you've heard of me. I'm looking for two men and a girl and we reckon they could have got off the boat here.'

Seated in the chair, Edmonton swung round to face them. 'They're here all right, Mr Keller,' he said, before Finlayson could speak. 'They came on the boat from New Orleans. What do you want with 'em?'

For a moment, Keller seemed on the point of ignoring him, instead swinging his gaze back to the sheriff. Then he said tersely, 'I don't see what this has to do with you, mister, but that girl is my future wife only she don't exactly see it that way at the moment. I'm here to take 'em back.'

He seemed to notice Edmonton's hand for the first time. His thin lips drew back across his teeth in a wolfish grin. 'Was it that man Darby who did that to you?'

'If you mean that gunslinger who was with the old man and the girl – yes. And I mean to get him. If you want him, you can have him after I've killed him.'

The hawk-faced man considered that for a moment, then glanced round at his companions. 'Seems we're both after the same thing, boys.' To Edmonton, he said, 'I only want the girl. The other two are of no interest to me so long as they're off my back – permanently.'

Swinging on the sheriff, he rasped, 'You got any objection to me and my boys searchin' the town for these three?' His tone implied that it made no difference to him whether the lawman agreed or not.

Finlayson nodded reluctantly. 'Like I told Edmonton here, we've only got the one hotel in town. If they ain't there, my guess is they figured you'd be coming and they're out among the hills yonder. If that's so, you won't find 'em in the dark. You'll have to wait until mornin' and I can let you have a posse to go with you.'

'I'll do that.' Turning on his heel, Keller gave orders to his men to check on the hotel, then moved back into the shelter of the boardwalk. Taking out a cigar, he lit it carefully, shielding it with his hands against the gusting wind and rain.

A couple of minutes later, Edmonton and his two companions came out, following the directions Finlayson had given them to the doctor.

Seated in the chair in the small room, Flint Edmonton cursed volubly as the doctor cleaned his smashed hand. He had already downed three large glasses of whiskey but it had done little to deaden the pain.

'You say somebody pulled a gun on you on the riverboat, Mr Edmonton?' The doctor, a small, balding man dipped the cloth into the bowl where the water was already stained a deep crimson.

'That's the way of it,' Edmonton growled. 'Some gunslinger by the name o' Darby got on at New

Orleans. Me and my friends were just havin' a friendly game o' poker with this old fellow when I was accused o' cheatin'. Naturally, I had to defend my honour and it was then that this gunman butted in.'

The doctor nodded, but said nothing, waiting for him to continue. He'd recognized the three men as professional gamblers the minute they had walked in. Inwardly, he could guess what had happened, but with men like Edmonton and the two well-dressed men standing near the door, it was better to keep one's mouth shut.

When there was no further conversation, he said, 'You told this to the sheriff?'

One of the other men said harshly, 'Naturally, the sheriff has been informed. We know the three of 'em came into town so they must be holed up some-where. There are men lookin' for them now.'

The doctor brought out two rolls of bandage. Tautly, he muttered, 'This is goin' to trouble you for some time, I'm afraid. Guess you won't be dealin' cards for a while.'

Edmonton uttered a harsh yell of pain as the doc moved his hand a little. 'Watch what the hell you're doin'.' His mouth drew down into a hard, tight line. 'Call yourself a doctor.'

For a moment, there was a sharp retort on the doctor's lips. Then he said calmly, 'You should be thankful there is a doctor in this town. This ain't New Orleans, you know.'

'All right, Doc. Just get on with it. I've got a score to settle with that *hombre* who did this.'

The doctor finished bandaging Edmonton's hand, then stood up. 'I guess I can understand how you feel, but you sure as hell won't be able to use a gun with that hand, not even a derringer. From what you say o' this man, it's lucky you weren't killed.'

Edmonton gave a mirthless smile. 'He'll soon find out he should have killed me. I only need one hand to pull a trigger and the next time, I'll make sure I have the drop on him.'

Motioning to Winton and Dawson, he pushed open the door and left. Outside, he noticed Keller still standing by the wall near the sheriff's office. He did not seem to have moved during the past twenty minutes.

Clem did not wake until shortly before dawn. For a moment, he felt disorientated, not sure of where he was. Then the events of the previous night came back with a rush. Thrusting himself up onto his elbows, he stared around. Amy and her grandfather were still sleeping.

Getting to his feet, he fumbled his way to the door. It was still securely locked but a moment later, he heard the soft sound of footsteps outside and the rattle of the key in the heavy lock. Drawing his gun, he stepped slightly to one side.

The door opened and the Negro came in, closing the door behind him. Putting the gun away, Clem asked tautly, 'Any trouble?'

He shook his head. 'That man Keller rode in last night with five of his men. They went to have a word with the sheriff.'

'I know. We saw them just before you arrived on the scene.'

'I kept watch on the street for a while. Keller and his gunmen drew a blank at the hotel and then checked all the stores along the street. They didn't see me but I heard him shout that they'd ride out with a posse to search the hills at first light.'

'And those three crooks? What o' them?' Colly had woken and overhead. 'They still in town?'

'Yessir. They is still here. They stayed at the hotel for the night.'

Hitching his gunbelt higher about his waist, Clem said thinly, 'Then we've got to get out o' this town before that sheriff rounds up his men and joins with Keller. We need three horses and—'

Before he could finish what he was saying, the door suddenly burst open. Finlayson stood there, a Colt in his hand. Stepping inside, he left the door slightly ajar so that a thin wedge of the early dawn light filtered in.

Savagely, Clem swung on the man. 'So this is a trap,' he rasped harshly. 'You do it for some reward?'

'This ain't a trap, Darby,' Finlayson said calmly. 'I'm not here to arrest you.' He glanced round to where Amy was struggling to her feet. 'I came to help you.'

'Help us?' Colly said. 'Why would you do that?

'From what we've just heard, a whole heap of folk have made charges against us. It ain't like a lawman to aid fugitives.' Suspicion still flared in Clem's mind.

'Let's just say I know somethin' of this man Keller.' Finlayson's sharp glance studied Amy's face as she stood in the shadows. 'He said he aims to take you back and marry you. Is that true?'

'Yes,' Amy nodded.

'So, from the way he said it, I reckoned you don't want to go back of your own free will.'

'He's the last man I'd agree to marry.'

'I thought so. It seems to me that what he meant to do amounts to kidnappin'. As for those other three men, I've seen their kind before; they're nothin' more than two-bit gamblers.'

'So how do you aim to help us?' Colly enquired.

'It'll be another hour before Keller's men and the posse are ready to ride out. Far as they're aware, you're all on foot so you can't get far.'

He turned to the Negro standing beside him. 'Sam here will come with me and we'll bring three horses. After that, you'll be on your own. Your best plan would be to strike east from here, around the cotton fields. Nobody will figure on you goin' that way. They'll all take the north trail out o' town and if they have to search for you along the way, it'll take 'em some time'

Glancing at Clem, he added, 'It'll cost you three hundred dollars for the horses and saddles. That's the best I can do.'

Colly dug into his jerkin. 'I reckon I got that from those critters in the poker game,' he said, counting out the bills.

A moment later, the sheriff and Sam slipped away into the pre-dawn darkness. Clem watched them move cautiously around the rear of the shanties, then closed the door.

'You think we can trust them?' Amy asked anxiously. 'Most of the sheriffs I know are in the pay of the big men.'

'I don't know. I hope so.' Clem was still dubious. 'We'll just have to wait and see.'

The minutes passed with an agonizing slowness. Then a faint sound reached Clem standing just inside the doorway. Opening the door an inch, he peered out. For a moment, he saw nothing.

Then he picked out the figure of the sheriff leading two horses around the rear of the shanties. Sam was behind him with a smaller mount.

'He's kept his word,' he said tautly, stepping back. 'We'd better make ready to leave.'

Less than five minutes later, they were riding along the edge of the cotton fields, heading in an easterly direction. Already, there was a faint yellow flush showing along the horizon ahead of them. As he rode, Clem threw an occasional glance over his shoulder but each time there was no sign of anyone following them.

Drawing alongside Colly, he said, 'You know anything o' this country?'

Colly pursed his lips before replying. 'Not much. My hunting ground was south along the river.' He cast about him for a moment. 'There doesn't seem to be any trail here. Could be the only one is that north o' the town and we daren't use that.'

Clem shrugged. 'Not unless we can reach it well ahead o' those men. I guess we'll just have to cut across country for a while and then turn north.'

CHAPTER IV

KILLERS ON
THE TRAIL

After thirty minutes' slow travel around the vast borders of the cotton fields, they came upon more open ground which had not yet been taken over for cultivation. Here, they made much better progress, letting their mounts set their own pace.

There was no sense in pushing the horses too hard. That way, they tired more easily and inwardly, Clem knew there might come a time when they would need every last ounce of speed and endurance from their mounts. As he rode, with his two companions a little way behind him, he scanned the terrain which lay ahead of them.

Somewhere to their left lay the only trail in this neck of the woods, that along which Keller and his men would now be riding. But as the sheriff had said, Keller would believe them to be on foot and he would have to search every possible hiding place.

Even then, they would have to be alert for an ambush; all of which meant they would have to travel at walking pace keeping a close watch on both sides of the trail.

Shortly before noon, as they topped a low rise, Clem brought his mount to a sudden halt, reining up sharply.

'What is it?' Amy's voice reached him from a few yards away. 'Trouble?'

'Could be.' He spoke without turning his head.

Down below was a small valley and to one side of it stood a long wooden shack. Smoke issued from a hole in the roof and there was a horse tethered to a rail in front of it.

Colly edged his mount forward a little way, peering down through slitted eyes. 'Maybe we could get some grub there and water. We ain't eaten for so long I'm beginnin' to ferget what food tastes like.'

'Could be we won't be welcome,' Clem warned. 'But I guess it's a chance we'll have to take.'

He set his mount to the downgrade. There was no one in sight as he rode up to the shack, but as he made to dismount, the door swung open abruptly and a tall figure stepped out. There was a shotgun in the man's hands and it was pointed directly at them.

'Don't bother steppin' down, stranger. If you make a move towards those guns, I'll send all o' you to hell.'

Clem raised his hands slowly. 'We ain't here to make trouble,' he said calmly. 'All we want is to buy some food and water. Then we'll be on our way.'

The man advanced slowly, not once lowering the

weapon in his hands. Clem saw that he was perhaps in his late thirties, tall and straight, and he guessed he had once been a soldier like himself.

'So you say.' He appeared to notice Amy for the first time for a look of surprise flashed over his lean features. 'What's a woman doin', riding with you?'

'She's my granddaughter,' Colly said, thinly.

'And you?' The shotgun swung a little to point directly at Clem.

'Clem Darby. I—'

'Lieutenant Clem Darby? You fought with Lee.'

Clem felt a twinge of surprise go through him at his words. 'I did serve under General Lee durin' the war.'

'Then you're welcome here, Lieutenant.' The other lowered the gun, waited until Clem had stepped from the saddle, then shook his hand warmly. 'The name's Shaun Ramsey. Sorry about the gun, but I had you figured for Northerners. They've been here before, carpetbaggers from back East, bringin' fancy lawyers with 'em from New Orleans. Step inside, all o' you. I'll soon rustle up somethin' to eat.'

He led the way into the shack and motioned them to sit at the long table. Soon, there were heaped plates of beans, potatoes and bacon in front of them. Ramsay waited until they were finished, standing by the window as if expecting trouble.

Sitting back in his chair, Clem asked, 'You been here long, Shaun?'

He turned. 'I came back after the war finished, though I spent some time with Quantrill.'

'You were with Quantrill's Raiders?' Colly asked, surprise on his face.

'Not for long. Some o' the things he did, I didn't agree with. When I left him, I came back here expectin' to find things just as they were before it all started.'

There was a deep bitterness in his voice. 'My brother got here a couple o' months before I did and found both our parents had been shot and everythin' burned down. You can see the ruins on the other side o' the hill yonder.' He pointed.

'And your brother?'

'He buried our father and mother but I guess he couldn't face all that had happened. He left before I got here, leavin' just a note saying he was headin' out. I've no idea where he is now.'

Amy glanced up from her plate. 'You're saying that the soldiers killed your parents and destroyed everything?'

'That's the whole truth of it, ma'am. I just stayed because there was nothin' left to do. I can't work the place on my own – just grow a few things for myself. I've often thought o' just riding out and headin' West, find a place a long way from here.'

'Why didn't you?' Clem enquired.

'I reckon when you've been in the army and made a lot o' friends, seen many of 'em die, the thought o' riding a lonesome trail just don't appeal.'

Coming back to the table, he lowered himself into a chair. He stared at Clem from beneath lowered lids. 'I can guess you're in some kind o' trouble. What is it, if you don't mind tellin' me?'

'You ever heard of a man named Keller?' Clem replied.

'Ed Keller? Sure, I've heard of him. They say he runs most o' New Orleans. Owns the biggest plantation in the territory. If you're runnin' from him you are in big trouble.'

'He's sworn to make me marry him,' Amy said. 'If I don't, he'll have my grandfather here arrested on some trumped-up smuggling charge and they'll hang him.'

Ramsay's face hardened. 'From what I hear, he has a lot o' dangerous men workin' for him and Keller is the most dangerous of 'em all. I can guess what you're up against.'

'I'm beginning to find that out for myself,' Clem muttered, rolling a smoke. 'He offered me a job as soon as I rode into New Orleans. When I turned him down, he threatened to have me killed.'

'He would,' Ramsay said heavily. 'If a man like yourself ain't on his payroll, he can't afford to have him walkin' the streets in case he throws in with his rival McFee. So where are you headed now?'

'North,' Colly put in. 'I got some business to take care of afore I die. Maybe I should've done it a long time ago.'

Pushing his plate away, Clem said, 'We'd like to thank you for your hospitality, Shaun, but we'd better be on our way. If you could see your way to lettin' us have some food to take with us, we'll willingly pay you for it.'

'No need to pay. You can have as much as you can carry. But why all the hurry? Ain't likely anyone will come here and there's plenty o' room for you to bunk down for the night.'

Clem shook his head. 'That's mighty good of you, but when we got off the boat last night, Keller rode in with five of his hired gunhawks. Not only that but Colly here had a run in with a trio o' crooked gamblers on the boat. He called one of 'em out for cheatin' and I had to put a slug into him.'

'You killed him?'

'No, just busted his hand a little. But they seem determined to get us as well. We figure our best chance is to pick up the trail well to the north and stay well ahead of 'em.'

Ramsay gave a nod. Going to the fireplace, he lit a taper and applied it to the end of his cigarette. Speaking through the thin column of blue smoke, he said soberly, 'Any of you know anythin' of this territory, where they could lay an ambush for you – or where you could lay one for them?'

As they shook their heads, he went on, 'I didn't think so. Like I said, I've been thinkin' of pulling out for some time. If you could do with an extra gun, I'll ride with you. At least for part o' the way you're going.'

'You mean you'd just leave all of this behind?' Amy asked, staring at him.

Ramsay's answering smile was merely a slight lift of his lips. 'What is there to leave? Just this old shack that's been my prison for the past four years.'

Colly hesitated for a moment, then nodded a grudging acquiescence. Clem could guess at the thoughts running through the old man's mind. He was still unsure of Ramsay and he did not intend to mention anything about Devil's Reach and the mine.

In a tight bunch, they rode out of the valley with Ramsay slightly in the lead. Clem was content to allow him to find his way towards the trail. Living here on his own all this time, he probably knew this territory like the back of his hand.

Inwardly, he did not share the old man's suspicions. Ramsay had recognized his name immediately, knew he had been a lieutenant in the Confederate Army. He had also noticed that whereas Colly had mentioned the name of Devil's Reach, he had said nothing about the mine. Clearly he meant to keep that information to himself.

A couple of miles further on they came upon more rugged land, dotted with long-spined cactus and mesquite. Rutted and slashed with wide cracks, it was difficult ground for the horses to traverse. Time and again, they were forced to make wide detours where cactus grew so thickly that it was impossible for their mounts to make any direct progress.

Then, shortly before nightfall, a dark smudge appeared on the horizon. Reining in his mount, Ramsay pointed and said harshly, 'There's the trail runnin' north from the river. If Keller and his bunch have been forced to ride slowly, lookin' for you, we should be several miles ahead of them by the time we reach it.'

With the sun dropping swiftly towards the west, they spurred the mounts to their limit, knowing that here, out in the open, they would be clearly visible to anyone riding that trail. Nevertheless, it was almost dark by the time they entered the fringe of trees bordering the wide, hard-trodden track.

Waving the others back, Clem dismounted and made his way cautiously through the trees. Slowly, he moved along the trail for several yards, studying it meticulously before going back to the others.

'If they are followin' the trail,' he said confidently, 'they're still between us and that town.'

'How can you be so sure of that?' Amy asked, leaning forward in the saddle.

'It rained durin' last night. Today, the weather has been dry and hot. If they had passed this way they'd have left the marks o' horses there. I've checked and there's nothing. I doubt if any riders have been this way for the past week or more.'

'Then I suggest we go on for a little while, keeping among the trees,' Ramsay muttered. 'That way we won't leave any trail for 'em to follow. Then we can find a place to camp. I also reckon we should set a watch through the night, just in case they do come this far. With Keller, you can expect anything once he's fired up.'

As they edged their way among the tall trees, Clem wondered about the girl. So far she had kept up with them, making no complaints. Whether she would still be the same by the time they reached their destination, he wasn't sure. It was going to be tough on them all but she would be the first to feel the strain.

Half a mile further on, they turned deeper into the trees, soon coming upon a small clearing. It was far enough from the trail to be well hidden but close enough for them to pick up any sound of riders passing by through the night.

Not daring to light a fire, they ate their food cold. There was little conversation during the brief meal. Not until they had finished did Ramsay say, 'I've been thinkin' about those men trailin' you. Maybe there's a way to head 'em off and send them along a false trail.'

'How do you figure on doin' that?' Colly asked tersely. 'It won't be easy to fool a man like Keller.'

Ramsay sat forward a little. 'The way I see it, we're some fourteen miles from the river. If they keep comin' they'll reach here some time through the night.'

'So?'

'So if I was to ride a way along the trail yonder and then head back I should meet up with 'em. They ain't lookin' for me, but if I was to tell 'em I'd seen you cutting away from the trees some hours ago and headin' south, it should be enough to send 'em in the wrong direction.'

Clem considered the plan for a while. As Ramsay said, there was nothing to connect them with him. 'It might work,' he agreed finally. 'But be careful. If Keller should suspect you're lyin', I don't give much for your chances.'

'I'm prepared to risk it,' Shaun said. Moving over to where the horses were grazing on the lush grass among the trees, he swung himself into the saddle, checking that the shotgun he'd brought with him was in the wide scabbard. A moment later, he moved silently away through the trees and disappeared from sight.

*

Riding beside Finlayson, Keller struggled to hold his irritation in check. They had followed this trail since morning, pausing every so often to examine the underbrush on both sides for any sign that anyone had passed through it. Now he was beginning to believe they were on a wild goose chase; that somehow those three had slipped through their fingers.

The men and horses were beginning to tire. Several of the riders in the posse were grumbling at the slowness of their pace and the incessant stops.

Yet even when the rain had stopped by early morning, it had failed to lessen the deep, burning anger within Keller. This was the only trail out of town and he felt certain his quarry had not left on the riverboat; not while those three tinhorn gamblers had watched the waterfront until it had left.

He knew they would have kept a strict watch, carefully checking everyone. Edmonton wanted these three just as much as he did. But either they were still holed up someplace in town, somewhere they had overlooked, or they had had help from someone and by now were miles away, heading through the hills. That last possibility grated within his mind and the sense of futility at this snail's pace of a pursuit was building up inside him into a tight knot.

Turning to Finlayson, he said angrily, 'This is getting' us nowhere. We've spent a whole day draggin' our feet along this trail without any sign of 'em. They could be twenty miles away by now and getting further away every minute.'

'Then what do you suggest we do, Mr Keller?' the sheriff said coolly. 'Ride hell for leather along this trail and maybe pass within a couple of feet of where they're hiding in the brush? They can't get far on foot and with a woman with 'em.'

From somewhere behind him, Edmonton called harshly, 'I'm figurin' they ain't on foot. Me and my two friends here had trouble getting horses this mornin'. Seemed to me there should've been more in the livery stables considerin' how many folk there are in that town back there.'

'You sure o' that, Edmonton?' Keller called back.

'Just seemed kind o' funny to me. Either they stole 'em, or they had help from someone.'

'Unlikely anyone would help 'em.' Finlayson put in. 'Seein' they'd just got off the boat, it ain't likely they knew anyone in town.'

'I'm not so sure,' Keller rasped thickly. 'If Amy Hutton got around to tellin' someone I intended abducting her and forcing her to marry me against her will, that could explain it. Somebody might have taken pity on her.'

He pushed his mount forward at a faster pace. To his men, he shouted, 'You men follow me. I ain't standin' around any longer. They're up ahead and I mean to—'

He broke off as Finlayson hissed sharply, 'Hold your horses. There's a rider up ahead, comin' this way.'

Swiftly, Keller pulled his Colt, holding it ready. A moment later, the lone rider appeared around a bend in the track. Finlayson saw the man rein up sharply as he noticed them.

'All right, mister,' he called sharply. 'Who are you?'

'Who wants to know?' Ramsay said.

Finlayson drew back his jacket, the star on his shirt dimly visible in the darkness. 'I'm the sheriff. I asked you a question.'

'The name's Shaun Ramsay. Just what the hell is this? You out lookin' for someone?'

'That's our business.' Keller gigged his mount and rode forward until he was barely two feet from him. He held his gun menacingly. 'You been on this trail long?'

Ramsay shrugged, keeping his hand well away from the shotgun. 'Two or three hours. Why?'

'We're lookin' for three people. One of 'em is wanted for attempted murder, tried to kill Flint Edmonton back there.' He jerked a thumb towards the band of men. 'You seen anyone while you've been ridin'?'

Ramsay scratched his chin. 'I did see three riders quite a while back. But I doubt if they're the ones you're after.'

'Why not?'

'Well, one of 'em was a woman. What would she be doin' with a wanted killer?'

'You're sure there was a woman with 'em?' Edmonton had ridden up and was staring directly at Ramsay.

'They were a ways off and riding fast, but there ain't nothin' wrong with my eyesight, mister. It was a young woman, well dressed.'

'It's them!' Keller said tautly. 'Did you see which way they were headed?'

Ramsay nodded. 'Reckon they must've cut off this trail. When I spotted 'em they were heading across country towards the hills to the south.'

'South?' Edmonton gave Ramsay a curious look. 'That don't make any sense. That way they'd be headed back towards New Orleans. The only way they've got a chance is to head north-west. Probably try to reach Twin Springs. That's the nearest town where they could hole up for a while.'

Finlayson uttered a short laugh. 'It seems you don't know much o' the country away from the river, Mr Edmonton. I reckon this man Darby, or that old fellow you say is ridin' with them, knows a lot more of it than you do. They'll figure that heading for Twin Springs is just what we'd expect them to do.

'By cuttin' south, they can swing around the hills and steer clear o' that town in a couple o' days. While you were hunting' for them, they'd be well away and you'll never catch up with 'em.'

Edmonton thought that over. There was a thin sneer on his lips as he retorted, 'Or he's trying to throw us off the scent with a double bluff.'

In front of him, Keller swung sharply in the saddle. 'Are we goin' to sit here arguin' all night? Goddamnit! We're wastin' precious time. This man's just told us the direction they went. I'm taking my men south. The rest o' you can do what you like.'

'What do you intend doing, Sheriff?' Edmonton asked thinly.

Finlayson shrugged. 'It won't help me and my

posse ridin' into Twin Springs. I've got no jurisdiction there. My guess is they're clear out o' the territory by now. I'm headin' back into town.'

'Suit yourself,' Keller snapped angrily. He gestured to the men at his back, almost knocking Ramsey from the saddle as he urged his mount past him. In a tight bunch, they swept along the trail, vanishing out of sight around the acutely angled bend fifty yards away. The sound of their mounts faded into swiftly fading echoes.

Glancing towards Edmonton, Finlayson said tautly, 'If you want my advice, mister, I'd forget about those three and go back to playing the suckers on the riverboats.'

Edmonton's face flushed at the rebuke. Then he lifted his right hand. 'Forget about this?' He shouted the words at the lawman. There was naked scorn in his voice. 'I'll hunt that two-bit gunman down if I have to trail him all the way across the continent. The same goes for that oldster who called me a card cheat. Neither of 'em are goin' to get away with it.'

'Then why didn't you ride with Keller and his bunch?' Finlayson asked. 'My guess is you'll need some guns to back your play if you do meet up with Darby.'

For a moment, the other squared up to the sheriff as he fought to control his fury. His hard features were twisted into a scowl of rage. Through thinned lips, he snarled, 'I'm heading for Twin Springs, ridin' through the night if I have to. Whatever Keller reckons, that's where they'll head for and I mean to be there before them.'

Pausing, he added, 'Could be I'll get more co-operation from the law there than I got here.'

'Guess that's your prerogative, Edmonton,' Finlayson muttered tautly, swinging his mount. He made to move back along the way they had come, then paused as the gambler called out, 'At least you can tell me the best way to Twin Springs, Sheriff.'

Finlayson's face hardened at the scornful emphasis the other put on the last word. Swallowing the rising anger in him, he said flatly, 'Follow this trail for a couple o' miles. Then you'll come on a narrow track leadin' over the hills to the west. Twin Springs is close on forty miles in that direction.'

Leaning forward in the saddle, Ramsay said quietly, 'You need me for anything more, Sheriff?'

Finlayson shook his head. 'You can go on your way, Ramsay. And thanks for your information.' Raking spurs to his sorrel, he signalled to the posse to follow him.

Edmonton remained fuming in the saddle for several moments, then edged past Ramsay. Pausing beside him, he said in a low voice filled with menace, 'If I ever discover you're deliberately sending us on a false trail, mister, I'll come lookin' for you once I've dealt with this gunhawk Darby and his companions.'

A faint smile touched Ramsay's lips but there was no mirth in it. 'Do that, friend. I ain't used this scatter-gun for quite a while but when I do, I never miss my target.'

For an instant, Edmonton seemed on the point of making a sharp retort, then noticed the expression on Shaun's face and thought better of it. Jerking savagely on the reins, he sent his mount bounding forward with Dawson and Winton following close behind.

Ramsay waited until the sound of hoofbeats had died away, then headed into the densely packed trees. Cautiously, he made his way back to where the others were camped.

Clem glanced up as he slid from the saddle. 'How did it go?' he asked softly.

Ramsay squatted down next to him. 'Better than I expected. I told 'em I'd spotted you riding for the hills to the south. Keller swallowed that but the *hombre* Edmonton reckoned it was a double bluff and you were cutting around that range and headin' for Twin Springs. Him and his two companions reckon they'll get there before dawn and lie in wait for you.'

'And the sheriff?' Colly queried.

'He's ridden back to town. Guess he figures you're well over the hills by now.'

Leaning back with his shoulders against a tree, Clem said, 'What do you know o' Twin Springs?'

Rolling a smoke, Ramsay lit it and drew deeply on it. He was silent for several moments. Then he pushed his hat back onto his head. 'I've been there on a couple of occasions. It was hit pretty bad by the North durin' the war. There ain't much law and order there.'

Staring into the darkness around them, Clem considered what he had said. Despite the fact that Keller had taken the wrong trail, he doubted if the man would pursue it for long before he realized he had been duped. The logical thing to do would be to ride across open country, by-pass Twin Springs and keep on going.

But the provisions they had brought with them would last for only a couple of more days. After that they would have to find more and that limited their choices. He grew aware that Amy was watching him closely out of the darkness.

'You're thinking that we'll have to ride to Twin Springs and take our chances with those three gamblers, aren't you?' she asked in a low voice.

He wasn't sure whether she saw his slight nod. 'It's the only choice we have. Sooner or later there's goin' to be a further showdown with them. Either that, or we'll always be lookin' over our shoulders.'

Colly yawned and flexed his shoulders. 'Leave that decision until the mornin', Clem. We're all tuckered out and need some sleep.'

CHAPTER V

TWIN SPRINGS

The next morning and most of the afternoon, they rode west. For the first half of the journey, they had ridden across wide grassland, crossed by numerous small streams. But gradually, the going had become rougher as they hit an out-thrusting tongue of the Badlands. Here the arid earth baked and simmered in the hot sun.

Sidewinders and scorpions abounded among the rocks, darting away at their approach. There was no sign of any trail, nor did they come across any indication that anyone had travelled this way in the recent past. Yet all the way they kept a sharp lookout for other riders.

Since the war, countless drifters rode these lands, some seeking work, others determined to get their hands on money any way they could; outlaws and gunslingers, holding up the stages and robbing the banks. Outlawry was rife and nowhere more so than in the south.

Yet they had seen no one. It was as if the whole world was deserted. By slow degrees, their shadows lengthened. Despite the fact that the sun was sinking slowly, the heat had remained, scorching their flesh, drying their throats until swallowing became an agony. There was now very little water left in their canteens.

Shortly after mid-afternoon, they came upon a narrow river. During the spring and autumn rains, it would be a raging torrent. Now there were only a couple of inches of water trickling sluggishly along the stony bottom.

Halting on the nearer bank, Clem said hoarsely, 'We'll rest up here for a while. With luck we should reach Twin Springs by nightfall.'

Helping the girl down, he asked, 'Are you all right?'

Brushing back a stray strand of hair from her face, she forced a wan smile. 'I'm fine. Don't worry about me. It's just this heat and dust.' She took down the canteen and uncorked it.

'Better go easy with that,' he warned. 'We still have a way to go and we can't drink that water down there.' He jerked a thumb towards the river. 'It's full of alkali. Just take a few sips and run it round your mouth before you swallow it.'

Sinking onto the hard ground, he rolled a cigarette and drew the smoke deep into his lungs. It hurt his parched throat but enabled him to think more clearly. He knew there would be trouble waiting for them once they reached the town and with Colly and his granddaughter tagging along it was going to make things even more difficult. Ramsay, he knew, was a man who could take care of himself.

But with a man like Edmonton, it was impossible to know what to expect. Men driven by greed did desperate things – and now the gambler had finally located Colly and those deeds, he would stop at nothing to get his hands on them. Whether he would be willing to share the spoils with his two confederates was something only time would tell.

Somehow, Clem doubted it. Once he, Colly and the girl were out of the way and the gambler had those deeds in his hands, Edmonton would be scheming how to avoid a three-way split. Undoubtedly, he had already made plans to get rid of his partners.

There was still Keller to consider, but if he kept to the route Ramsay had given him it would be at least another day before he reached the town, circling around the range of hills to the south.

Half an hour later, they were back in the saddle, fording the river. On the other side, the ground was just as barren and dry. Here and there, great balls of tumbleweed rolled across it, driven on by the gusting wind that blew from the south. The range of low hills which had stood across the horizon for the past couple of hours was now so close they readily made out the narrow pass through it.

Pointing, Ramsay said hoarsely, 'Twin Springs is less than a mile or two beyond that pass. I reckon we should move more cautiously now. This close to town, there might be other folk around.'

'You think Edmonton might have guessed we'd

head this way?' Colly asked.

'It's possible,' Clem put in sharply. 'He won't dare to meet us face to face. Men like him shoot from shadows. But even with his two friends, he can't watch the town from every direction. Almost certainly, he's already spun some yarn to the sheriff here, warnin' him there's a wanted killer headed this way.'

Riding through the pass, they paused at the end. In the near distance, they made out the town, nestling in a narrow valley. In the deepening dusk, a few lights were already showing. Even from that distance, Clem recognized that Twin Springs was a fairly large town, far bigger than the last one they had visited.

To one side, he could just make out large cattle pens and guessed this was beef country. But it was still a frontier town and undoubtedly full of the lawless breed.

Urging his mount forward several yards, he scanned the terrain in their immediate vicinity. Already, an idea was beginning to form in his mind. He was aware that the others were watching him closely.

'Somethin' on your mind, Clem?' Colly asked, as he rode back.

'Somethin' I learned durin' the war,' he replied with a grim smile. 'I figure we should reconnoitre this place first before we all go ridin' in to find out if those three are here and, if so, exactly where they are right now.'

He swung his glance from Amy to her grandfather.

'There's a wide gully yonder. I want you to conceal yourselves there while Shaun and I check everythin' out.'

'Now see here,' Colly retorted thinly, 'I ain't hidin' from those cardsharps. I—'

He broke off as Amy laid a restraining hand on his arm. 'Clem's right, Grandfather. You're a stubborn old fool, but this time, listen to him.'

'Damnit! I can still use this rifle and—'

'Sure you can, old-timer,' Clem said evenly. 'But I ain't takin' your daughter into that town until I'm sure we can find some place where she'll be safe. You don't want to leave her here all alone, do you?'

Finally, Colly simmered down a little. 'All right,' he conceded grudgingly. 'We'll wait here until you get back.'

'Now you're showin' some sense,' Clem said, pulling sharply on the reins and setting his mount to the downgrade with Ramsay close at his heels.

Approaching the outskirts of the town, they slowed their mounts to a walk. Sitting tall in the saddle, Clem took in everything in a single, all-embracing glance. There were two wide streets, inter-secting each other at right angles near the middle of the town. Here was a large square, ringed by tall buildings.

Now that darkness was falling, lights showed along all of the streets. The sound of music came from several of the saloons and, judging by the number of horses tethered to the rails, Clem guessed that all of these places were well frequented.

'Leastways, I doubt if we'll have much trouble

spotting those three coyotes,' Ramsay said out of the corner of his mouth. 'This has the look of a cattle town to me.'

'So far east?'

Ramsay grinned. 'That was good grassland we crossed before we hit the alkali. Reckon they'll have an advantage over the others much further to the west. They won't have far to drive their herds to market.'

'All right,' Clem said tautly. 'We'd better see if we can find Edmonton and his two companions. At this time o' night, they'll probably be in one o' the saloons tryin' to cheat some o' these men out o' their money. We'll split up here. That way it'll take less time.'

Nodding, Ramsay turned his mount to the side of the street, got down, and looped the reins over the rail. He waited until Clem had done likewise, then pointed along the boardwalk. 'I'll take this side. You check the other – and watch your back. Those cardsharps know you. Far as I'm concerned, I'm just the man they met along the trail.'

Crossing the street, Clem paused with his hands on the batwing doors, throwing a quick glance inside. The saloon was full. All the tables were occupied and there were several men standing at the bar. However, there was no sign of the men he was looking for.

Going up to the bar, he ordered a drink. Sliding a bottle and glass across the counter, the bartender asked casually. 'You just ridden in, mister?'

Clem gave a brief nod. 'I'm lookin' for three

friends o' mine,' he replied evenly. 'They rode in ahead o' me.'

'Plenty o' men come into Twin Springs.' The other threw an appraising glance at the Colts in Clem's holsters. His eyes narrowed down a little and he made an elaborate gesture of wiping a couple of glasses.

'Guess I'll find 'em at a poker game somewhere. They came off the riverboat a couple o' days back. One of 'em you can't mistake. A big man with a busted hand.'

The unmistakable sound of chairs being scraped back caused Clem to turn sharply. Four men had risen to their feet and were moving towards him. The leader held his hand close to the gunbutt at his waist. There was an ugly expression on his swarthy features, his lips drawn back across his teeth.

'Did I just hear that you're a friend o' that sidewinder Edmonton?' he snarled viciously.

'You know him?' Clem asked thinly.

'Sure we do,' grated a second man. 'We caught him with a couple of aces up his sleeve after he'd cheated us out o' more'n a hundred dollars. Should have killed him or run him outa town.'

'Only he seems to have some pull with the sheriff,' grunted a second man. 'But I don't reckon that goes for you, mister.'

Clem swallowed the rest of his drink before saying, 'If you figure I'm in cahoots with those men, you've got it wrong.' he said slowly. 'This *hombre* Edmonton tried to kill a good friend o' mine on the riverboat. Guess you've seen what I did to his hand.'

'You did that to him?' There was now a note of uncertainty in the first man's voice. He glanced round at the three men standing behind him. Finally, he muttered, 'Then I guess we got you wrong, friend.'

'Do you know where I can find those three critters,' Clem asked tightly. 'I've got a score to settle with 'em.'

Before any of the four men could speak, the bartender butted in. 'They put up at the Lost Trail hotel, mister. But right now, I reckon you'll find 'em in the square at the Golden Nugget saloon. There ain't any other place that'll have 'em.'

'Thanks.'

As he stepped towards the door, the bartender said harshly, 'I wouldn't try any gunplay unless you want to find yourself in the jail. Like we said, he's got some pull with Sheriff Lister.'

'I'll keep that in mind,' Clem replied.

Pushing open the doors, he stepped out into the street. It had not occurred to him that Edmonton might be known so far from his usual haunt on the river. That made things more difficult than he had thought. Doubtless where the sheriff was concerned, money would talk and, provided there was no killing and Lister got his share of the profits, the lawman would be prepared to turn a blind eye to their other activities.

Stepping down from the boardwalk, he ran his glance along the dusty street. There was no sign of

Ramsay. Ignoring the curious glances he got from several of the folk on the boardwalks, he made his way quickly to the square.

The Golden Nugget saloon occupied one corner, separated from two others by narrow alleys. Pausing, he watched as a small handful of men rode up from the opposite direction. He waited until they had gone inside before edging towards the doors.

Ramsay was standing at the bar, his back to him. Clem lifted his hand to push the door open, then stopped as some instinct warned him to stay where he was. From the edge of his vision, he spotted the movement on the far side of the room.

Three men stepped into view and he sucked in a harsh breath as he recognized them immediately. They were Edmonton and his two companions. All three had guns in their hands as they moved towards Ramsey.

Slowly, Clem moved to one side, drawing his Colt. He glanced quickly around the square. At the moment, it was empty.

Inside the saloon, there was a sudden hush as Edmonton called sharply. 'You there at the bar. Ain't I seen you somewhere before?'

Ramsay turned slowly to face him. He allowed his glance to drop towards the derringer in Edmonton's uninjured hand. 'What is this?' he asked. 'I don't know you. Guess you're mistakin' me for someone else.'

Edmonton grinned wolfishly. 'I never make a mistake. You're the one we met on the trail.'

Shrugging his shoulders, Ramsay said, 'So I met you on the trail. You got some problem with that?'

Edmonton stepped forward a couple of paces, his features twisted into an ugly scowl. 'Somehow, I've got the feelin' that meeting you there was mighty convenient; too convenient for my likin'.' He turned slightly towards his companions. 'Ain't that right?'

'My guess is that he's in with those three, Flint,' Winton agreed. 'Could be they're somewhere in town, which is why he deliberately sent Keller and his men on a wrong trail, reckonin' we might go with 'em.'

'That right, mister?' Edmonton lifted the gun slightly, lining it up on Ramsay's chest, his finger hard on the trigger.

'You know damned well it ain't,' Ramsay muttered. 'I just told you what I saw.'

'I reckon that ain't good enough.'

Before Ramsay could say anything more, Edmonton fired, the shot racketing loudly in the room. Ramsay reeled back against the bar, slumping to the floor, as Clem thrust the saloon door open and stepped into the room.

All three men swung round in unison. Before they could bring up their weapons, Clem's Colt spat gunflame. Winton stood for a moment, teetering on his heels as the heavy slug took him in the chest. Then he spun sideways, smashing into the nearby table. A couple of feet away, Dawson was on his knees, struggling to hold himself up, his eyes wide and staring.

Swiftly, Clem swung on Edmonton, triggering off two shots. Both missed as the other man hurled himself down onto the floor. Out of the corner of his eye, Clem saw the bartender thrust himself upright. The shotgun in his hands swung swiftly in Clem's direction.

Only split-second reflexes saved Clem's life at that moment. Without pausing to think, he threw himself backward, and crashed into the swing door, rolling onto his side on the boardwalk. Splinters of wood flew past his head as the shot hammered through the air where he had been standing. Pushing himself hard against the wall, he gritted his teeth, and hauled himself to his feet.

Getting his legs under him, he hurled himself inside. A surge of anger went through him as he realized there was now no sign of Edmonton, who had taken advantage of the bartender's action to slip out of the back.

Grimly, Clem swung the Colt to cover the men seated at the tables. 'First move any o' you make for your guns will be the last,' he said grimly. 'That goes for you too,' he added viciously, throwing a glance towards the man behind the counter. The bartender's features were ashen as he dropped the shotgun onto the counter.

Glancing down at Ramsay, Clem saw that he was dead. Blood stained the front of his shirt and there was no life in his eyes.

'He made a try for that scattergun,' muttered the barman sullenly. 'We all saw how it was. Edmonton fired in self-defence.'

'Like hell he did.' A savage fury forced fierceness into Clem's voice. 'I saw everythin'. This man was shot down in cold blood. His gun is still across his shoulders.'

'Don't reckon there's any way you'll get a jury in Twin Springs to take a stranger's word against the testimony o' so many witnesses,' said one of the men at the nearest table. 'Reckon if you value your life, mister, you'll get out o' town fast before the sheriff arrests you for the murder o' these two.' He indicated the bodies of Dawson and Winton.

Through tightly clenched teeth, Clem rasped, 'If any o' you see that snake Edmonton, tell him he's just made the biggest mistake of his life. He'll pay for this night's work just as those two have.'

With a swift movement, he thrust himself through the doors, a hot anger riding him. With an effort, he forced calmness into his mind. He now knew just what kind of town Twin Springs really was; a nest of gamblers, gunhawks, with a crooked sheriff on the take. It would not be long before word of this reached Lister as the sound of those gunshots would have been heard clear across the square.

Thrusting the Colt back into its holster, he walked swiftly along the street. Already, there was the sound of shouting at his back and people were running in the direction of the square. Making himself as inconspicuous as possible, he finally reached the place where his mount was tethered.

Pulling himself into the saddle, he put the horse to a swift gallop. Unless he missed his guess, there would soon be a posse on his trail and whatever happened, he did not want to lead them to Amy and her grandfather. Edmonton had got away, but there was no chance he would go very far, not with the thought of those deeds in Colly's possession.

Sooner or later, he would make an attempt to get his hands on them and now, with his two confederates dead, there would be no need to split that mine three ways.

Reining up on top of the rise, he turned his mount and glanced back in the direction of the town. From his vantage point, he could make out details clearly in the wide swathes of yellow light cutting across the street. There was now plenty of activity going on with riders gathering in front of the nearest building.

As he had expected, the sheriff had been alerted and a posse was being hurriedly assembled. Maybe they figured it would be quite easy to follow his trail and hunt him down. Smiling grimly to himself, he swung his mount off the trail, heading into the tall pines to his right. What they hadn't figured on were the lessons he had learned while in the army, guerilla tactics used when they had been hunted down by the Northern soldiers.

Here the ground was in his favour. Low branches overlooked the narrow track which led steeply up towards the high summit. In places, there was tangled brush lying across the path. Deliberately, Clem put his mount through it, leaving clear tracks. Where the tree branches overhung his trail, he made sure several of them were snapped by his shoulders as he pushed through them.

By the time he attained the summit there was a

trail which a blind man could follow on a dark night. Now he picked out confused shouting at his back, harsh cries as the riders came upon the trail. Smiling a little to himself, he waited for a moment, then pushed his mount hard into the brush on the downward slope.

After travelling for a quarter of a mile, he reached a place where the track widened abruptly. Here, he halted, then turned his mount, working his way quickly back to the turn-off. Hauling back on the reins, he set the animal to the steep drop-off.

Fortunately, the sorrel was a sure-footed brute, picking its way cautiously around scattered rocks, often sliding straight-legged for several yards before finding surer ground.

At the bottom, a narrow stream gushed through the dense undergrowth, racing over a rocky bottom. Once on the other side, he pushed his mount into a thick tangle of tall bushes, bringing it to a sudden halt.

The sound of riders was much closer now, a couple of hundred feet above him. Parting the stiff branches, he squinted up along the slope and a moment later, made out the shadowy figures. They were riding hard, clearly following the trail he had laid. Directly above him, he saw the man in the lead lift an arm and point straight ahead.

A few moments later, they swung away in a tight line, heading deeper into the trees. Letting his breath go in a long sigh, he waited until the sound of hoofbeats died away, then turned his mount and moved quickly away into the darkness. It would be some time before those men realized they had been fooled. By then, he would be several miles away, following a circuitous route back to where Amy and her grandfather would be waiting anxiously.

CHAPTER VI

TROUBLE TRAIL

It was more than half an hour later when Clem approached the narrow pass, coming on it from the eastern end. Overhead, the sky was completely dark, scattered with a multitude of brilliant stars. To the east there was a faint flush that heralded moonrise.

Quite certain that he had thrown off the posse from Twin Springs, he had nevertheless kept a sharp watch on his trail but there had been no sign of any pursuit. Somehow, he reckoned the sheriff would return to town once the trail he was following ran out but there was still the possibility he would get more men together and scour the hills after daybreak.

Reaching the end of the pass, he reined up and glanced about him. The next moment, a figure stepped out of the shadows, a rifle lined on him. He recognized Colly at once.

'Put that rifle up, Colly,' he called softly. 'It's me – Clem.'

Colly stepped forward with Amy close behind him,

and gave a quick glance towards the pass. 'Where's Ramsay? Ain't he with you?'

Stepping down, Clem shook his head. 'Ramsay's dead, shot down in cold blood by Edmonton.'

'The hell you say.'

Clem saw the old man's hands tighten on the Winchester.

'What happened, Clem?' It was Amy who spoke, a look of deep concern on her shadowed features.

Briefly, Clem told them all that had happened in Twin Springs, finishing with how the sheriff there was in league with the gamblers and had led a posse after him for the shooting of Edmonton's two companions.

'Then you didn't get that two-bit crook.' There was barely controlled anger in the old man's voice.

'He must have slipped away through the back o' the saloon when that bartender took a shot at me. But, make no mistake, this ain't the last we'll see of him. So long as he thinks there's a chance of getting his hands on those deeds o' yours, he'll stick to us like glue.'

'Then if I ever get him in the sights o' my rifle he won't bother us any more,' Colly muttered. 'I rather liked Ramsay. In my book, he was a straight *hombre*.'

'Guess we all thought that,' Clem replied. 'But right now, we have to get out o' here. Come sun-up that sheriff might decide to head out this way, particularly with Edmonton on his back. I'd also hoped to get us some provisions in Twin Springs, but I guess we'll just have to go hungry for a while.'

Glancing in Amy's direction, he asked, 'You feel

up to ridin' through the night?' He could sense the weariness in her.

'I'll be all right,' she said, with a trace of iron in her voice. 'But I'm worried about the horses. They've been carrying us all day and—'

'We've got no choice,' her grandfather said sharply. Walking back, he tightened the cinches under both mounts and pulled himself wearily into the saddle, thrusting the Winchester back into its scabbard.

The night had been long and bitterly cold. The clear, starlit sky had sucked all of the heat from the ground so that the temperature had dropped dramatically. During the long hours, they had swung in a wide arc, well away from Twin Springs.

By the time the dawn brightened they had left the town far behind them and were traversing a long stretch of bare, rocky ground. All three of them were swaying in the saddle with utter weariness. Their mounts too were almost at the limit of their endurance, their necks drooping, struggling to keep up more than a bare walking pace.

Tall hills lined the northern horizon but these were more than twenty miles distant and Clem knew that once the sun rose and with it the heat head, there would be no shade in this barren land where they might find some shelter.

'How much further can we go like this?' Amy asked, struggling to speak through dry, caked lips.

Clem jerked up his head to glance at her. He realized he had almost fallen asleep in the saddle, his head dropping forward until it almost rested on his chest. Rubbing his eyes, he focused his gaze on her, noticing the lines of strain and utter exhaustion etched across her face.

Opening his mouth to make some kind of answer, he suddenly swung his gaze over her shoulder. There was something there in the distance, something that was not easy to make out in the glare of the dawn. Lifting one arm, he pointed stiffly.

Beside him, Colly mumbled something through his parched throat as he followed the direction of Clem's pointing finger. Then he got the words out. 'That's a wagon train, Clem. Looks like they're just getting' ready to break camp.'

Swallowing on his dry mouth, Clem said hoarsely, 'If we're lucky, we can get some water and provisions from them.'

Raking spurs to their mounts they somehow managed to get an extra burst of speed from the weary animals. As they drew nearer, Clem saw that there were perhaps thirty wagons in the train with both horses and oxen in the traces. It was clearly a well-organized group which meant that there would be a number of outriders with it on the watch for marauding Indians and outlaws.

When they were still almost half a mile from it, two men broke away from the wagons and rode swiftly towards them. Slowing their mounts to a walk, they waited until the men came up to them. Both were hard-faced individuals, clearly gunmen hired for the job of protecting the train.

Keeping his hands well away from his sides, Clem

urged the sorrel forward. He saw both men throw a surprised look in Amy's direction, saw them relax visibly. The first man said tautly, 'What would you be doin' in this wilderness? Not runnin' from the law, I hope.'

'Not unless you call Sheriff Lister in Twin Springs the law,' Clem said calmly.

He saw the look which passed between the two men; an enigmatic glance which he couldn't analyse. Hastily, he went on, 'We don't mean to bring any trouble to the folk in that wagon train. All we need is water and some provisions. We're ready to pay for anything you can let us have.'

'You'd better ride back with us and have a word with Jim Clark, the wagon-master.'

Shrugging, Clem acquiesced and followed the two men in silence. His mention of Lister had brought some reaction from these men, but he was unable to guess what it meant.

Riding towards one of the wagons, one of the men called sharply to a large, burly man seated on the tongue.

'These three are lookin' for water and vittles, Mr Clark. We figured they'd better talk to you. It seems they've had a run in with Lister back in Twin Springs.'

Clark lowered himself from the tongue of the wagon and walked towards them, then came to a halt, his hands on his hips, looking them up and down with a penetrating gaze. There was both suspicion and a hint of hostility in his stance and the set of his jaw.

'Just Lister?' There was a sharp, speculative expression in the other's eyes as he ran his keen gaze over them. 'Somehow, I reckon there's more than that polecat of a sheriff on your trail.'

'Just what do you mean by that?' Colly retorted.

'A couple o' nights ago we ran into a bunch o' gunslingers back east,' Clark replied. 'I recognized one of 'em as Ed Keller. He said they were looking for a woman ridin' with two men, both of whom match your descriptions. They forced us at gunpoint to stand by while they searched the whole train. Reckon they must want you three pretty badly.'

'It's me they want,' Amy said dully. 'Ed Keller has sworn he'll marry me, even against my will. If I don't agree, he'll have my grandfather here hanged on some trumped-up charge of smuggling contraband into New Orleans along the Trace.'

'That so?' The big man rubbed his chin thoughtfully. 'Well, I guess that changes things a little. I never did go along with men forcin' women to marry them against their will, however rich and influential they might be.

'As for Lister, he's no lawman. He's only the sheriff there because he allows cardsharps, crooked lawyers and gunhawks to run the town.'

He motioned towards the wagon at his back. 'I reckon you're all dead on your feet. We'll get you somethin' to eat and drink. Then you can sleep in there. Ain't likely anyone will come lookin' for you again. You can ride with us as far as you like.'

'Thanks, friend.' Clem slid gratefully from the saddle. Every limb ached and he could scarcely stand as cramp bit deeply into his legs. Helping Amy down, he held her for a moment as she struggled to remain upright.

Two of the women came forward from one of the wagons with bowls of soup and bread. 'We've only just broken camp,' one of them said. 'The stew is still warm.'

Clem accepted the bowl thankfully, spooning the thick stew into his mouth. He ate ravenously, chewing on the bread. The dryness of his throat made it difficult to swallow but somehow, he got it down with sips of water.

When he had finished, Clark came over with a bottle of whiskey. 'This might help to keep it down,' he said. 'Then you'd better sleep. If there is any trouble, I reckon we'll be ready for it this time.' He paused, then added, 'Just how far are you headed? Not that it's any business o' mine, but—'

'North-west,' Clem replied. 'A place called Devil's Reach.'

'That's one hell of a way,' Clark muttered. 'Must be close on two hundred and fifty miles.'

'You've heard of it?'

'Heard of it – sure. But that's outlaw country. It ain't no place to take a woman.'

'I got business there I should've taken care of seven years ago.' Colly put in.

Clark shrugged as if to say it was no concern of his. Then he jerked his thumb towards the big wagon. 'There's room in there for the three o' you. Leave your mounts. We've got feed for them. Once we get the animals in the traces, we'll be movin' out.'

There were rugs in the back of the wagon. The floor was hard but to the three of them it felt like a benison as they stretched themselves out. For a few moments, Clem lay there listening to the shouts of the men and the noisy yells of the children. Then he was asleep. Even the bumping, rocking motion of the wagon some twenty minutes later, as they moved off, failed to waken him.

When he did wake it was several hours later, well into the afternoon. Beside him, Amy and her grandfather still slept and, moving carefully so as not to waken them, he eased himself onto the tongue beside Clark.

Rolling a cigarette, he lit it, blowing the smoke into the air. By now, the hills were much closer and in front of them, the trail was easy to follow. It was clear that several wagon trains had used this route in the past.

'How far are you takin' these folk?' he asked

Clark spoke without moving his head. 'Clear to California. This is the second one I've taken in the last five years.'

'Any trouble the last time?'

'There's always trouble,' commented the other. 'Especially along the Camino Real once we cross the Sabine. That's a real breedin' ground for outlaws. But this time we're ready for 'em as you can see for yourself.' He jerked a thumb towards their rear. 'And every man with the train, and most o' the women, knows how to handle a gun.'

Leaning sideways, Clem glanced back. There were at least a dozen outriders spread out along the line of wagons, hardened gunmen with their hands never far from their rifles.

'I'm glad you decided to trust us.'

'Out here, it ain't wise to trust anyone. If you hadn't got the woman with you and we hadn't met up with Keller back along the trail, you might have been shot by now. I've known o' men joinin' up with wagon trains, only to turn out to be in cahoots with a bunch of outlaws waitin' further along the trail.'

Clem nodded briefly. 'I get your meanin',' he said, tossing the cigarette butt away. 'If you've no objection, we'll stick with you until we cross those hills yonder. I still ain't sure that Lister won't bring a posse after us.'

Clark drew his lips back from his teeth. 'We'll take care of him if he does,' he said meaningfully. 'I've had a run in with that crooked lawman myself. As for Keller, you can be sure most o' these folk are still smartin' at the way he held us up at gunpoint. They don't take too kindly to men like that. They're the kind o' men these people are hopin' to get away from.'

'I can understand that,' Clem agreed. 'I served with Lee in the Confederate Army. Once the war ended, I thought things might return to something like normal. Instead, I find land-grabbers everywhere, bringing in hired guns to enforce their own laws.'

'Then why don't you head for California with us? From what I've heard and seen, it's a brand new country, just opening up. Men like you would make a good livin' there.'

Clem gave a taut smile. 'That was the way I had it figured before I met up with the old man and his granddaughter. Guess I got kinda attached to them.'

For a moment, there was also a smile on Clark's face. 'You could do a lot worse, my friend,' he said, his tone full of meaning.

That evening, the wagon train camped on high ground just a few miles from the hills which now dominated the skyline to the west. The sky had remained cloudless all day and even in the shade of the wagon, the heat was suffocating. All around the camp, the dust hung like a grey curtain, settling only slowly in the still air.

A short distance away was a small stream, providing them with all the water they needed. Most of the children were splashing in it, washing off the clinging dust. Branches had been lopped from the trees bordering the steam and four fires had been lit.

Seated with his shoulders against a tall slab of rock, Clem stretched his legs out to their full length. It had been a long, jolting ride but the sleep and food had refreshed him. In the distance, Colly was in deep conversation with Clark but there was no sign of Amy.

A few moments later, however, she came into view between two of the wagons, saw him sitting there, and walked over. Her face bore a serious expression. Seating herself beside him, she remained silent for several moments.

Then she said flatly, 'Have you heard this talk about Devil's Reach – that it's outlaw country.'

'I've heard it.'

'Do you think it's true – I mean that it's much worse than most other places?' She drew up her knees and sat with her arms clasped around them, her head bent forward a little.

He knew she was seeking some kind of reassurance from him but there was little he could give. Finally, he said softly, 'I guess they don't call it Devil's Reach for nothin'. It's bad country, full o' small trails that lead nowhere. There are countless places where men on the run from the law might hide and hold out against an army.'

Staring out into the night, she sat for a while, scarcely moving, obviously turning his words over in her mind. Then she leaned back looking directly at him. 'I've tried to persuade my grandfather to stick with this train, forget about that gold mine and go on to California. The wagon-master is willing to let us stay but Colly will hear nothing of it. He's so goddamned stubborn, says that strike is his and he's doing this for his partner who died out there.'

'I reckon I can understand how he feels. It's not just the thought of losin' something which is rightfully his and which he wants you to have – it's the idea that he might just as well find Edmonton and hand those deeds over to him.'

'I'm afraid I don't see it that way. Even if he gets there without being killed, it'll take years before he gets that gold out and all the time there'll be Edmonton on his trail. You know as well as I do that man will never give up. But he's too stupid and mule-headed to realize that.'

114

'You'll never change him,' Clem said tautly. 'But there is one thing I'm afraid of.'

In the faint firelight he saw her turn her head to look directly at him. Her eyes were bright in the dimness. 'What's that?'

'Taking you along with him. He reckons he can take care of himself after all those years in the forest, but—'

'I think he's finally realized that,' she interrupted. 'He wants me to stay with this train and travel with them all the way to California. Once he's worked his claim to his mine and made his fortune, he'll find me somehow.'

Inwardly, Clem knew that this would be the best thing to do, but he also knew that she was just as determined as her grandfather and he said nothing.

After a few minutes, she rose to her feet and moved towards the wagons. 'Maybe he'll be thinkin' more clearly in the mornin',' he called after her. 'I'll have a talk with him then.'

After she had gone, he got to his feet and moved nearer to one of the wagons, closer to the fire, spreading out his blanket on the ground. The night air held a chill and above him, the stars were so bright they seemed close enough for him to touch them. There was scarcely any sound in the camp now.

A horse snickered somewhere in the distance but this was the only noise to disturb the stillness. Rolling onto his side, he stared at the fire. Fresh twigs and brush had just been piled onto it. Now the flames were licking along the branches, crackling slightly as they burned the sap inside.

His mind was a riot of confused thoughts and vague premonitions. He found himself thinking about Flint Edmonton, nursing his injured hand, filled with the lust for gold and the burning desire for vengeance.

That man, he thought, was more dangerous than Keller. For nearly eight years, he had sought Colly, searching for him across Texas and then to New Orleans. Now he had found him, only to let him slip through his fingers. For a man like the gambler that would now become an all-consuming obsession, driving him on where other men might have turned back and cut their losses.

With these thoughts chasing each other around inside his head, he finally fell asleep, only to be rudely awakened by a hand shaking him by the shoulder. He was instantly alert, reaching for the Colt beside him.

'Easy, Darby.' Clark was kneeling beside him. 'There are riders coming. Could be either Keller or that sheriff from Twin Springs. Either way, you'd better get outa sight among these rocks. Your two friends are already there. Don't make a sound and leave this to me.'

Scrambling to his feet, Clem swiftly made for the rocks and edged his way among them, finding Hutton and Amy crouched behind a large boulder, out of sight from anyone below. Dropping onto his knees beside them, he eased his Colt from its holster and checked that all of the chambers were full.

Through a narrow gap in the rocks, he could make out details among the shadows below him

116

where the yellow moonlight threw a net of light over the wagons. Lifting his glance he could just discern the bunch of riders spurring their mounts towards the camp.

As they approached, he recognized Edmonton, his bandaged hand hanging limply by his side. For a moment, the burst of anger inside him was so strong that before he realized it, he had lifted the gun in his hand to sight it on the gambler. He caught himself just in time as the riders reined up, one man pushing himself to the front.

The bright moonlight glinted off the star on his shirt. Down below, Clark moved out of the shadows.

'You the wagon-master o' this train?' Lister called, in a harsh, authoritative tone.

'That's right,' Clark replied. 'What's your business with us at this time o' night?'

Clem saw the other stiffen abruptly in the saddle. 'I'm Sheriff Lister of Twin Springs. We're trailin' a wanted killer, man by the name o' Darby. We figure he may be headed this way.'

'Get on with it, Lister.' Edmonton bit the words out, twisting a little in the saddle to scan the wagons drawn up in a wide circle. 'That murderer shot down my two partners in cold blood.'

'That's right,' Lister said harshly. 'Mister Edmonton here has sworn out a warrant for his arrest and we mean to take him in. If he is ridin' with you, hand him over now and there'll be no trouble.'

'We aim to get him, even if we have to search every wagon in this train,' Edmonton cut in.

'You ain't searchin' anything,' Clark said thinly

with a note of menace in his voice. 'You may reckon you're the law in Twin Springs, but out here, as far as this wagon train is concerned, I'm the law.'

Lister leaned forward a little, his face suffused with anger. 'You're makin' a big mistake, mister,' he grated thinly. 'If you refuse to co-operate with the law, you'll maybe think twice when you're behind bars in the jail.'

'I know exactly what your so-called law is like, Lister,' Clark said tautly. 'Try a man yourselves, set up a rigged jury, and string him from the nearest tree before any circuit judge gets into town. Even if this *hombre* was here, I wouldn't hand him over to your kind o' justice.'

'Search the wagons,' Edmonton said shrilly. 'If anyone makes a move to stop you—'

Clark braced himself with his legs apart. 'I wouldn't advise any of you to make a play for your guns. Right now there are more'n twenty rifles trained on you. One move my men don't like and you'll all get a bullet where you won't like it.'

From his hiding place, Clem saw the riders turn their head slowly, then move their hands equally slowly until they were resting on their pommels. The bright moonlight glinted on the rifle barrels of the men standing in a wide circle around them.

'You won't get away with this.' Edmonton choked on his words, his face twisted into a scowl of utter fury. 'You'll be hunted down by every lawman in the country.'

Clark uttered a harsh laugh. 'You don't scare me none with your threats. The next time I see you, or any o' those men with you near this wagon train, I'll most likely mistake you for a band of outlaws and order my men to shoot on sight. Now, turn your broncs and ride out while you're still in the saddle.'

For a moment, it seemed that Edmonton's savage rage was about to get the better of his natural caution. His good hand seemed poised to strike for his gun. Then, swallowing hard, he switched it to the reins, jerked his mount around with a vicious tug.

Beside him, Lister threw Clark a glance full of malevolence before doing likewise. In a tight bunch, the men rode away, not once looking back. Clem waited until they were nothing more than a dwindling dot in the moonlight before he climbed down from the rocks.

'Guess we owe you a debt o' thanks,' he said to Clark. 'Those men could be dangerous.'

The wagon-master shrugged. 'I've seen men like that come and go. They hide behind a badge to enforce their own laws, or those given to 'em by men like Edmonton. I'll have a couple o' men keep watch through the rest o' the night, just in case they should decide to come back.'

CHAPTER VII

UNHOLY ALLIANCE

Seated at one of the tables in the Golden Nugget saloon, Flint Edmonton was in a foul mood. A blind fury seethed inside him, gnawing at his vitals. Already, the bartender had felt the lash of his tongue when he had brought over the bottle of whiskey and a glass.

Angry thoughts chased each other through his mind. That yellow-livered-sheriff had as much backbone as a worm. If he had called that wagon-master's bluff instead of backing down, those three fugitives would be safely locked up in the jail by now. Instead, he had simply ridden off with his tail between his legs like a whipped cur.

Inwardly, he was sure that Darby and the other two were somewhere in that wagon train, probably believing that he had finally been beaten. Swallowing the last of the whiskey in the glass, he called harshly for another bottle. Gritting his teeth, he swore savagely under his breath, then glanced up sharply as the batwing doors were thrust open and a bunch of riders came in.

They looked travel-stained as if they had travelled far without pausing for much rest. He gave them only a cursory glance, then looked again with a shock of surprise as he recognized the big man in the frock coat.

Thrusting himself back in his chair, he called loudly, 'Mister Keller, bring your men over here, the drinks are on me.'

Keller walked over and lowered himself into the chair facing the gambler. Finally, he gave a brief nod with little of welcome in it. 'You been in Twin Springs long, Edmonton?' he asked, pouring whiskey from the fresh bottle into his glass.

'Long enough to know where those three are right now – and that you can expect no help from the sheriff here. We could have got them four hours ago but he allowed himself to be faced down by a bunch o' nesters.'

Keller turned his head and threw a quick, enquiring glance around the room. 'Where are your two friends?' he asked.

Edmonton's mouth twisted into a grimace. 'Dead, both of 'em. Shot down by that killer Darby.'

'That so?' Keller drew his lips into a tight line. 'Reckon if you can't trust the law here, you don't have much chance of gettin' them on your own.'

'Mebbe not. But if we were to join forces. . . .'

Keller smiled but it was merely a slight twisting of his lips. 'Why should I help you?'

'Because it's the woman you want. I want the other

two – and I know exactly where they are and where they're headed. You could spend weeks scouring the Badlands and never find 'em. With my help, you'll have the girl by this time tomorrow.'

Keller rubbed at the dust which covered his cheeks. There was a crafty look in his eyes as he said, 'There's somethin' about this I don't understand. So you want to kill this man Darby for what he did to your hand and maybe for shootin' down your two confederates.'

Leaning forward, he fixed the other with an unwavering stare. 'But what's the old man to you? I've known about Hutton for years, just an old recluse living in the woods. Since he never interfered with my business along the Trace, I left him alone. He was no danger to me.

'Yet from what I've heard, you deliberately enticed him into a game o' poker, let him win a few hands, then somehow forced him into callin' you a card cheat so you had a lawful reason to draw on him.'

Edmonton thought fast, wondering just how much Keller knew about Hutton. He felt reasonably sure the other knew nothing of those gold-mine deeds. That was something no one knew about, except perhaps the old man's daughter and Darby.

'I never laid eyes on him before that day he came aboard the riverboat from New Orleans.' Somehow, he forced a sly smile. 'Sure I meant to take him for all he had. He was just as big a sucker as the rest o' them. But no man calls me a cheat and gets away with it. If he'd kept his mouth shut like the others did, none o' this' – he lifted his bandaged hand –

'would've happened and my two friends would still be alive.'

Keller continued to stare for several minutes, then sank back, apparently satisfied. Nodding, he said slowly, 'All right, Edmonton. We'll join with you. But no tricks, or you'll go the same way as your two companions.'

'There'll be no tricks, Keller.' He gave a faint smile. 'How could there be? You've got all those men at your back. I'm just one man.'

Keller got to his feet. He stood for a moment, looking down at the other man, then said quietly, 'We've been on the trail for two days. Be ready here in the square at dawn tomorrow. Then you lead us to them.'

'I'll be here.' Edmonton watched the men leave with a satisfied smile on his lips. Things were beginning to turn out better than he had anticipated less than an hour before.

Sitting loosely in the saddle, Clem watched as the last of the big wagons rumbled past him, the metal chains clanking like individual pistol shots. The journey through the hills had been long and tortuous and there had been inevitable delays whenever they had encountered rockslides which had almost completely blocked the trail.

The decision to leave the train here had been a hard one to make, made even more difficult by Amy's inflexible decision to continue travelling with her grandfather and himself. All attempts to persuade her to remain with Clark and the settlers had failed.

They waited until the long line of wagons had almost disappeared into the distance, shrouded in a slowly dissipating cloud of yellow dust, then Clem turned to face Colly. 'You sure you know where we go from here?' he said sharply.

'North-west.' Colly pointed. There was a look of concern on his wrinkled features which Clem noticed at once.

'You've got somethin' on your mind, Colly,' he said sharply. 'Whatever it is, spit it out.'

Colly hesitated, then said harshly, 'Up ahead of us, about five miles, is the Camino Real. It ain't just bad country to cross but they reckon there are more outlaws each mile than anywhere else in the territory except Devil's Reach, full o' men who either deserted durin' the war, or headed there just after it finished.'

'And you're deliberately leadin' us into it. What kind o' fool are you?' There was a distinct note of anger in Clem's voice.

'Goddamnit! There ain't any other way unless you want to backtrack for twenty miles and then swing north. Besides, all they're watchin' out for are the wagon trains that sometimes use this route. We ain't got anythin' they want.'

'No? What about that piece o' paper you're carrying?'

Hutton gave a toothy grin. 'They ain't goin' to find that,' he declared emphatically.

'Then let's hope you're right, because our lives may well depend on it.'

Two hours later, they came within sight of a great ridge of red sandstone which, at its highest point, lifted several hundred feet above the surrounding mesa. It stretched clear across the horizon, cutting them off completely from whatever lay on the other side.

Staring at it, shielding his eyes against the glare of reflected sunlight, Clem sucked in a harsh, dry breath that burned his throat.

'We're supposed to cross that?' he muttered, incredulously.

'There's a way,' Colly replied, pointing towards the northern edge. 'But apart from these outlaw bands, not many men know of it. Guess that's why those critters picked it for their hide-out. Nobody in their right mind would go up there after 'em.'

Clem ran a finger down the side of his nose. 'I don't like the idea either, especially with Amy here.'

'I've made it so far,' she retorted with a resolute expression on her face. 'I guess I can make it the rest of the way.'

In a tight bunch, they rode across the arid land, kicking up spurts of white dust behind them. Unerringly, Colly led them towards a massive overhang where tumbled blocks of stone lay balanced haphazardly on either side. Incredibly, there was a trail there, one so narrow that it seemed impassable even for a single rider.

Colly's mount snickered anxiously as he edged it towards the stricture in the rock. The girl followed with Clem bringing up the rear. On either side, the walls were so close they scraped the saddle-bags as they passed through. Coaxing the animals, they progressed with a painful slowness up the steep incline.

An hour passed with only their sun-thrown shadows accompanying them. Then, with an abruptness which took them unawares, the rock wall on their left came to an end. Below them, the drop was almost vertical, falling precipitously for more than a hundred feet.

Clem tightened his grip on the reins as a wave of vertigo swept through him. He had not realized they had climbed so high.

Colly's voice reached him a moment later. 'Don't look down. Just kept your eyes fixed straight ahead and you won't feel so bad.'

With a wrench of neck muscles, Clem did as the other suggested, fixing his eyes on Amy's back just a few feet in front of him. Sweat gathered on his back and shoulders. How the girl succeeded in controlling herself, he couldn't guess.

Here, there was no vegetation of any kind – but there were plenty of huge boulders where a man could conceal himself and lie in wait for anyone foolish enough to attempt this crossing. Without moving his head, Clem flicked his gaze in all directions, alert for any movement among the shadowed rocks.

But nothing happened until they reached the summit. Here, the ground was relatively flat and the plateau wide enough for them to halt their mounts and sit in a loose bunch.

Speaking through his teeth, Colly said, 'Reckon we should wait here a while and give the horses a chance to rest. The descent should be—'

He broke off sharply at a sudden sound. The next moment, before Clem's hand could reach the gun at his waist, four men had risen from the surrounding rocks, rifles trained on them. 'Step down from your mounts and keep your hands where we can see 'em,' one of the men said, harshly.

Once they had obeyed, he came forward slowly, his rifle pointed directly at Clem, obviously recognizing him as the most dangerous of the three. Pushing the weapon forward until the barrel ground into Clem's chest, he stared hard into his face. Then he stepped back a couple of paces, a curious expression in his eyes.

There was an incredulous note in his voice as he said, 'Clem Darby? I figured you'd ridden east after Lee surrendered.' Turning, he addressed the men at his back. 'This is Lieutenant Darby, boys. You remember him.'

Lowering the rifle, the other threw an awkward salute. 'Sergeant Seth Saunders, sir.' He gestured towards the others. 'Hal Cordell, Ben Iliff and Reb Meredith. You saved our lives that night when the platoon was ambushed near Savannah.' He grinned. 'So we meet again, Lieutenant.'

Clem forced himself to relax. 'The lieutenant tag ended with the war, Seth. Right now, we're tryin' to get through to Devil's Reach.'

'And there's somebody on your trail, is that it?' When Clem paused, he went on, 'Nobody crosses the Camino Real without a good reason – and that's the best reason I can think of'

'You don't miss a thing, do you?' Clem answered, nodding.

A few feet away, Amy said suddenly, 'These men

are outlaws, Clem. Yet you know them.'

'Outlaws, yes, ma'am,' Iliff said stiffly. 'But not entirely by our choice. We were all soldiers in the Confederate Army, fighting for what we believed in. When the war finished, there was nothin' left for us. The Yankees had burned and destroyed all of our homes and lands. Now we take what we can get.'

'So now you live outside the law.' There was an expression of understanding on Colly's bluff features. 'Reckon I can't blame you for that.'

Changing the subject, Saunders asked, 'How do you figure on getting all the way to Devil's Reach, Clem? You say there's someone on your tail; if they know where you're headed, they'll not stop until they catch up with you.'

'Guess we'll just have to face that when it comes.'

Saunders threw a quick glance in the direction of the other three men, then he let his gaze drift back to Clem's face. 'If you need any help, me and the boys will head north with you. Nothin' to keep us here and it'll be just like it was in the old days.'

'Besides, we owe you somethin',' Cordell butted in. 'You saved our lives that night. Guess we'd all be dead if it wasn't for you.'

Clem thought that over. He knew that, outlaws or not, these were men he could trust and sooner or later, Edmonton and possibly Keller would catch up with them. Four extra guns would certainly stand them in good stead.

'What do you think, Colly?' he asked flatly.

Hutton hesitated and Clem could see he was still dubious. At length, however, he said grudgingly, 'If

you can vouch for 'em, Clem, I ain't got any objec-
tions. Might be some trouble though if we were to
head into a town where there are wanted posters out
for 'em.'

'Ain't any out for us,' Iliff said harshly. 'We robbed
a couple o' banks back east, but we learned a lot
durin' the war and nobody saw our faces.'

'Weren't anybody killed and we figure it was no
worse than the way those Northerners robbed us of
our land and homesteads,' Meredith put in. 'Only
difference is that they are called businessmen and we
get the name of outlaws.'

It was four days later when they rode into a small
frontier town which, from the name on a wooden
sign, was called Sherman Forks. It had been four days
of hard riding across barren country, of blistering
heat through the hours of daylight and bitter cold
whenever the night fell. In the company of Saunders
and his men, they had crossed swiftly fflowing rivers,
swimming their mounts against vicious currents,
eaten their meals around blazing fires with the eternal silence pressing in on them from all sides, broken
only by the wild cries of coyotes.

Now Clem let his glance wander over the twin rows
of wooden buildings that flanked the narrow street.
In all, there were barely a score of them. Sherman
Forks looked like a town which had been started and
then forgotten, left to moulder and decay.

Several men were lounging on the boardwalks,
eyeing them with sullen, suspicious stares as they
dismounted in front of the only two-storey building.

It was obviously a hotel of some kind but there was no sign over the door, yet somehow, it had an air of solidity about it which all of the others lacked.

Going inside, Clem threw a swift glance about him. At first, he thought the place was empty. Then, walking towards the chipped wooden desk, he noticed the man sleeping in the high rocker chair near the far wall. Taking out his Colt, he hammered loudly on the desk with the butt.

Stirring himself, the old man rubbed his eyes for a moment, then got shakily to his feet. His eyes were wide as he stared at the gun in Clem's hand. Then he swallowed thickly, his Adam's apple bobbing nervously in his scrawny throat.

'You got any rooms for the night?' Clem asked mildly. 'For all of us?'

'Sure thing, mister. You can take your pick. We got nobody stayin' here now. Don't get many folk comin' through Sherman Forks. A couple o' prospectors now and again, comin' down from the hills.'

'We'll also need somethin' to eat,' Saunders put in. 'It's been a long ride.'

'Of course. I'll get you somethin' rustled up right away.' The man moved quickly towards a door on his left, opened it, and called something. A moment later, an old woman appeared in the doorway.

The proprietor said something to her in low tones, then came back. 'My wife will fix you something in ten minutes, folks. Just go through the door yonder.'

Following the direction of the man's pointing finger, Clem opened the door, his eyes still alert for trouble. There were three tables spread with white cloths and chairs set around them. Lowering himself into a chair, Clem stretched out his legs to ease the cramp in his muscles.

As he leaned back, Colly said sharply 'You seem a mite jumpy, Clem. You expectin' trouble here?'

'Could be. If not from those men outside, I can't forget Edmonton and Keller. There ain't any doubt that Edmonton knows where you're headed and if he's pushed his mount to the limit, he could have reached here before we did.'

'One man against six of us.' Meredith spoke up from the next table.

'There's also this man Keller and he's got a bunch o' roughnecks ridin' with him,' Colly muttered. 'If Edmonton has linked up with them, it might be a different story.'

Cordell grinned wolfishly and glanced round at his companions. 'Then I guess they don't know what they're up against – right, boys?'

All three men nodded in unison. 'We're in this fight with you, Lieutenant,' Saunders said. He made to say something more but at that moment, the door opened and the food was brought in.

The next morning when Clem stepped outside the hotel, there was a thin drizzle seeping from an overcast, leaden sky. A cold wind was blowing from the north, whipping in gusts along the narrow street. A couple of feet from where he stood, an old, whiskered man sat in a battered rocker, easing himself slowly back and forth.

As Clem built a smoke, the oldster said in a wheezing tone, 'Guess you and your friends are headed for Devil's Reach.'

Turning, Clem asked tautly, 'How would you know that?'

The other gave a cackling laugh. 'Hell, mister, there ain't no other place you can go.' He jerked the hand holding the battered pipe towards the far end of the street. 'Trail yonder only goes as far as the old prospectin' town o' Devil's Reach. No other place you can go unless you aim to climb them hills.'

'You know anythin' about Devil's Reach?'

Twisting his toothless mouth into a faint grin, the old man said, 'Far as I know there ain't many go there now, not like in the old days when there were plenty o' men diggin' there for gold. Now they reckon it's all worked out. Funny thing though, you're the second bunch o' men come ridin' into Sherman Forks headed that way.'

Clem jerked up his head at that remark. 'You meant some other band o' men have come this way?'

'Rode through in the early hours. Seemed in a mighty big hurry, too.'

Clem walked over to stand beside him. 'Did you see anythin' of 'em?'

'Sure thing. I don't sleep much at nights. Guess I see most o' what happens here. There was quite a big bunch o' men. Looks like frontiermen to me, all carryin' guns, except for two of 'em.'

'You notice anything odd about either o' these two others.'

The old man squinted up at him out of rheumy eyes. He puffed vigorously on the pipe for several seconds before answering. 'Reckon there was something strange about one of 'em. Had some kind o' bandage around his right hand. I figured someone had shot him in a gunfight.'

There was a pause, then he asked, 'Those men friends o' yours?'

Clem shook his head. 'Not exactly, but thanks for the information, friend.'

Going back into the lobby, Clem called the others together. 'Seems I was right about Edmonton and Keller. They rode together through the town some hours ago, headin' for Devil's Reach.'

'Then they're ahead of us,' Colly put in tersely.

'Looks that way,' Clem replied grimly. 'At least we won't have them at our backs. The sooner we're mounted up, the better.' He glanced at Hutton. 'How far is it from here to Devil's Reach?'

Hutton pursed his lips thoughtfully. 'Not far – ten or twelve miles.'

CHAPTER VIII

DEVIL'S REACH

It was easy to see why the place had been named Devil's Reach, Clem thought, as he surveyed the territory into which they were riding. They had ridden only three miles out of Sherman Forks but now the terrain had changed completely. Bad as the trail from the town had been, now it was nothing more than a track only a couple of feet wide, meandering seemingly aimlessly between high, needle-shaped rocks and long, low ledges.

Here and there, other narrow tracks led off to left and right, seeming to go nowhere. Now, forced to ride slowly in single file, it would be the easiest thing in the world for Keller and his band, concealed high in the rocks, to pick them off one by one. With nowhere to turn, they would be caught like rats in a trap.

From somewhere behind Clem, Iliff called softly, 'You sure you know where you're goin', old-timer?'

Colly's voice came back a few moments later, 'I

134

know this place like the back o' my hand. Trust me.'

'It ain't you I'm worried about,' Clem said harshly. 'Even though Keller and Edmonton can't be sure where we are, it'd be like them to have a couple o' men with rifles posted somewhere in these rocks.'

'Not here, it wouldn't.' Colly's voice sounded unduly confident. 'There's no way even a mountain goat could get up into them rocks. If there are lookouts, they'll be further on where the rocks break up.'

'I hope you're right.' Clem didn't share the old man's confidence. Ever since entering this narrow, twisting trail, there had been an itch between his shoulder blades. It was warning sign he had learned never to ignore.

A couple of miles further on and the enclosing rocks opened out slightly. The trail turned into a wide, shelving mass of smooth rock that dipped downward slightly. Below them, lay a wide stretch of flat, open ground.

All around them, however, sharp-edged rocks and clawing pinnacles of stone provided excellent hiding places for men with rifles. The little itch in Clem's back suddenly got worse.

Edging forward until he was beside Colly, he said tersely, 'I don't like the look of that ground down there. Too easy for us to be seen.'

Colly screwed up his eyes as he lifted his head to scan the surrounding rocks. 'Reckon this is going to be the most dangerous bit until we reach the mining town,' he observed, 'but there's nothin' else for it.'

Compressing his lips into a tight line, Clem remained silent for a moment. Then he said harshly,

'If there are any of Keller's men in those rocks, the only way to flush 'em out is to draw their fire.'

'You're not going to ride down there, are you, Clem?' There was a note of shocked anxiety in Amy's voice. 'That would be sheer suicide.'

'Can you think of a better way?' Turning to the others, he said tautly, 'Spread out among these boulders and have your guns ready. Somehow, I don't think Keller will leave more than one man to watch this trail. Up there, one man could pin down an army without exposin' himself to any return fire from this trail.'

He waited until Saunders and his three companions had moved quietly away into the rocks on either side. He knew these men of old, adept at moving silently whatever the nature of the terrain. If a man was concealed there, he would be dead before he knew anyone was close by.

Easing the Colts in their holsters, he gigged his mount forward. Now that he was out in the open, he felt the tension mounting swiftly in his mind. At any moment, there could be a man crouching among the rocks with a rifle trained on him, a finger tightening on the trigger.

At the bottom of the slope, he sat further forward in the saddle to present a more difficult target for any concealed marksman. He deliberately kept his gaze fixed on the ground directly in front of him giving the impression he was unaware there might be gunmen all around him. Some fifty yards away, a deep trench had been cut into the rock.

It looked too smooth and regular to be a natural

formation. Perhaps, he mused, it had been made by some of the old prospectors, possibly trying to find water in the godforsaken place. Tightening his grip on the reins, he turned his mount to skirt around it.

The next second, the bark of a distant rifle reached him and he heard the wicked hum of a bullet as it passed within an inch of his head. Without pausing to think, he grabbed the rifle from its scabbard and threw himself from the saddle. His shoulder hit the rim of the trench and, twisting quickly, he dropped into it. Fortunately it was less than four feet deep and there was a thick layer of dust and sand at the bottom.

Going down onto his knees, he thrust himself hard against the side, lifting his head slowly. Meticulously, he ran his gaze over the rocks to his left where he guessed the killer was holed up. Nothing moved.

A full minute passed and then he caught a fragmentary glimpse of movement. He saw it only for a brief moment and couldn't be sure whether it had been a man, or just his imagination.

Lifting the rifle, he thrust it onto the rock in front of him. A split second later, a second slug struck the dust less than four inches from him. Flinching, he forced himself to ignore the fact that the gunman had him pinned down. His keen gaze caught the faint puff of smoke close to a massive boulder on the far rim of the stretch of open ground.

The man was hardly visible, crouched inside a deep cleft in the rock. In the second he realized it would be impossible to get the guman with a direct shot, his mind had already come up with another tactic. It would not be easy but it was the only chance he had.

Taking careful aim, he sighted the rifle on the rock just to the right of the hidden bushwhacker. Swiftly, he loosed off three shots in rapid succession. For a moment, he thought he had missed the spot he was aiming for. Then, almost in slow motion, the man tumbled forward, hung there for an instant, then fell outward, his body turning over twice before he hit the ground fifty feet below.

Grinning viciously, Clem waited, but the man did not move. At least one of the ricochets had hit him in the side of the head. If it hadn't killed him outright, at least the fall would have finished him.

When there was no further fire from the rocks, Clem pulled himself out of the trench and signalled to the others. A few moments later, they came riding towards him, reining up sharply as they reached him.

'That was a stupid thing you did, Clem,' Amy said tightly. 'You could have been killed drawing his fire like that.'

'Never mind that now,' her grandfather admonished. 'We can expect a lot more trouble before this is finished. I've got to get to the assay office before those critters start stealin' my gold.'

Half an hour later, they came within sight of the old prospecting township. About a mile away the hillside rose vertically for hundreds of feet, enclosing a wide, flat stretch of ground covered with lengths of rusted metal tracks. Long wooden shacks stood haphazardly in crooked rows.

Irregular black holes, like vacant eye sockets, had

been hewn or blown by gunpowder out of the hill-side but there now appeared to be no activity down near the rockface. Closer at hand, however, stood the small township of Devil's Reach; mostly lop-sided shacks with a sprinkling of more modern buildings.

'If this is where you and your partner made your strike, there doesn't seem to be much goin' on now,' Clem said, as they reined up at the edge of the trail. 'You sure this is the place?'

Colly nodded emphatically. 'This is it. Yonder is the assay office where we registered our claim.'

Swinging on Saunders and the three other men, Clem said harshly, 'Since we know Edmonton and Keller have already got here before us, I suggest you four circle around and conceal yourselves in those rocks. Better take Amy with you. I'll ride down with Colly.'

Nodding agreement, Saunders gave a signal to his companions. Amy made to protest, but this time her grandfather overruled her. 'I'll be fine with Clem here. I don't want you in the thick of it if it comes to gunplay.'

Putting their mounts to the steep downgrade, Clem and Colly rode into Devil's Reach, eyes alert for trouble. Clem's initial surmise that the township was deserted was soon proved wrong. Several men stood on the rough boardwalk fronting a line of shacks.

Sliding from the saddle in front of the assay office, Clem followed Colly inside. So far, there had been no sign of the men who had been following them.

A small, bald-headed man stood behind an iron grille across the counter on the far side of the small room. He looked up enquiringly as they approached.

Taking the piece of paper from his pocket, Colly thrust it beneath the grille. 'I've come to work my claim,' he said briefly. 'My partner died o' fever some years ago but as you can see, I'm still around.'

The man examined the paper minutely, then handed it back. 'Sorry, Mr Hutton, but I'm afraid that claim ain't worth the paper it's written on.'

'What the hell do you mean? You tryin' to tell me it's worthless?' Colly expostulated fiercely, thrust his face up close to the grille. 'It's all there, all done legally.'

'This claim is more than seven years old and—'

Leaning forward, Clem said, in a cold, even voice, 'Are you sayin' that if a claim ain't worked within a certain length o' time, it's invalid?'

The clerk swallowed nervously before shaking his head. 'No, mister, I ain't sayin' that. I'm sure that everythin' written down there was done legally.'

'Then what is it you're tellin' me?' Colly demanded. For a moment, he seemed on the point of lifting his rifle and thrusting the barrel through the grille at the other.

Starting back a little, the man said hoarsely, 'You'll see that this claim you have is registered in two names – Colly Hutton and Ned Randers.'

'That's right. Ned was my partner. We rode out here some eight years ago and prospected this place together.'

The man held up his hands. 'What I'm tryin' to say is that a man showed up this mornin' just as I was openin' up. He claimed his name was Ned Randers and that his partner had died more'n seven years ago and now the claim belonged to him. Since he knew exactly where it is, well away from all o' the others, there was no reason for me to doubt him.'

'You remember what this man looked like?' Clem asked. Inwardly, he knew the answer before the old man spoke. 'Tall, thin *hombre* with his right hand bound up?'

'That's him,' the clerk affirmed.

'Edmonton,' Colly said thinly through tightly clenched teeth. 'And now he's laid claim to my strike.'

'Then I guess we'll have to change that,' Clem said, tersely, with a ring of iron in his voice. He led the way to the door and paused for a moment to survey the muddy street. He recognized none of the men he saw lounging on the rickety boardwalk.

'Where is this strike o' yours, Colly?' he asked brusquely.

'It's quite a way around that ridge yonder, well away from the rest.' Colly pointed.

'Then I guess that's where we'll find Edmonton and the others. From here we move real careful. They'll know we ain't far behind 'em and they'll have posted more men to watch the trail. We'll leave the horses here; they'll pick them up a mile away. I reckon it would be better if we were to go on foot.'

A grim fury rode Clem now, making him feel cold inside. The brazen way Edmonton had tricked his friend told him all he wanted to know about this man; a man driven by greed and the desire for gold. This made such men dangerous.

He smiled grimly to himself. There was one thing Edmonton had overlooked. In their desperate need to get here first: Edmonton and Keller had made a mistake. They had unwittingly ridden into a trap. There was no way out of the place except by this narrow trail.

Reaching the solitary shack which stood on the very edge of the wide, flat area, Clem risked a quick look around. At first, he could see nothing but massive rocks piled one on the other and a narrow track which angled to his right, cutting a thin slice of shadow through them.

Then a slight movement caught his eye. A brief orange flare showed a moment later. It was the light which came from a match. There was a man up there, almost completely concealed within a crevice in the rock, smoking a cigarette while he kept a close watch on the ground below.

Pulling his head back, Clem hissed, 'Like I figured, they've got a lookout posted on the ledge yonder. He's got a clear view from there. There's only one way to get him. Give me five minutes to get into position, then you make a dash for those rocks.'

Nodding to show that he understood, Colly crouched down beside the wall of the shack, the Winchester steady in his hands. Moving back, Clem worked his way around the side of the building, edging towards the rear.

A double line of rusted rails ran across the ground a few yards away. A little to one side, a wagon stood on them. Three of the wheels were no longer on the axles and it lay canted at a precarious angle. Most of the wooden sides were nothing more than a splin-tered, warped mass, but at least it would provide him with some cover.

Getting his legs under him, he thrust himself forward, weaving from side to side. Reaching the wagon, he crouched there for half a minute, then sprinted across the uneven ground, throwing himself down against the rocks on the far side.

He had expected to hear the sound of a shot, but none came. Quickly, he pulled himself up into the tumbled mass of boulders, finding handholds where there seemed to be none. A minute later, he came out onto a ledge which overlooked the mine work-ings some thirty feet below.

Narrowing his eyes, he ran his gaze over the rocks below him. At first, he could make out nothing. Then a slight movement caught his attention. The man's shoulder was just visible above a smooth rim of stone to his left.

Slowly, he eased the Colt from its holster. Further down, he made out the squat shape of the shack. A further minute passed, then Colly appeared, running quickly for the rocks. In the same moment, the gunman lifted himself, bringing the rifle up to his shoulder as he squinted along the barrel, aiming for the running man.

'Press that trigger and you're a dead man,' Clem said loudly.

He saw the gunman tense, saw his shoulder drop fractionally, knew he was trying to make up his mind whether to bring down his target, or meet the danger at his back. For a moment, Clem thought the killer intended risking a shot at Colly.

Then the man whirled swiftly, swinging his rifle in a wide arc to bring it to bear on Clem. He had almost turned when the gun in Clem's hand spat fire. For a moment, the man remained standing on his feet as he tried to summon up his last ounce of strength to lift the rifle.

Then a thin trickle of blood came from the side of his slackly open mouth and he arched back, his body following the rifle as they both bounced down the sheer rockface.

Standing inside the irregular opening in the rock, Flint Edmonton lifted the lamp they had found in one of the shacks and held it close to the moisture-dripping surface. A few feet away, Keller's tall form was a dim shadow in the gloom. He watched closely as the gambler moved slowly along the wall of rock.

Several thoughts were chasing each other through his mind at that moment. His suspicions about Edmonton had started during their brief meeting in Twin Springs. The gambler had asserted that he only wanted revenge on Darby after that shooting on the riverboat.

Had that been the only thing, he might have believed him. But his insistence that the girl and her grandfather were of no interest to him had been a little too insistent, too vehement. It had started him thinking that perhaps, Edmonton was more interested in the old man than he was in Darby.

Accordingly, when they had found no sign of them with that wagon train they had intercepted the following day, and Edmonton had insisted they should ride north-west, he had asked questions of the men riding with him. From two of them he had learned about Devil's Reach, an abandoned gold mining region, now reputedly worked out.

Mulling over that information, it had been an easy step to work out exactly what the gambler was after. Somehow, he had discovered that gold was still there to be had and Hutton held the key to it. Now, after insisting that he should accompany Edmonton into the assay office, his suspicions had been amply confirmed.

Lowering the lamp, Edmonton moved further away. Smiling grimly, Keller called, 'You found anythin' yet?'

'Nothin'.' His voice echoed eerily from the confining walls. There was a pause and then he went on, 'You're sure we won't be surprised by Darby and the others? If they trap us in here, we're finished.'

'There's no chance o' that. I've got two men spaced out along the trail and the rest of the boys are watching the entrance.' He knew that Edmonton was aware of this, that he also knew one of the men had a rifle trained on him every moment, just in case he did go for the derringer he carried. Keller trusted the gambler no more than he would a rattler.

Even though they had reached an agreement to split any gold they found, and there was an uneasy truce between them, he knew that Edmonton was already struggling to find a way to kill him. Probably he also knew that he had walked into a trap and there was no way out for him.

A moment later Edmonton uttered a low exclamation. Picking his way over the heaps of fallen rock, Keller moved over to him. In the light of the lamp, he saw where it was reflected in places from the rock. A dull shine, but still brighter in the lamplight than the surrounding rock.

'The old fool was right,' the gambler muttered harshly. 'There are nuggets here almost as big as your fist. No wonder he finally decided to come back. There's a fortune here if we can get it out.'

'I'll get a couple of the boys to bring some picks,' Keller said. He moved back to the entrance, then stopped abruptly.

From the dimness at his back, Edmonton called harshly, 'Just hold it right there, Keller. If that gunslick in front of you makes a single move, you get it in the back. You'll die before I do. Now tell him to drop that rifle.'

Keller cursed himself inwardly. The sight of the gold had momentarily distracted his attention from the gambler and he had inadvertently stepped between Edmonton and the gunman keeping an eye on him.

Moistening his lips, he said thinly, 'You know, you're an even bigger fool than I took you for, Edmonton. Even if you kill me, you'll be dead before you step outside these workings. There are six more men out there. You don't have a chance.'

Edmonton thinned down his lips. 'I'll have more chance than with you. I said, tell that hireling of your to drop his rifle and his gunbelt. This derringer can put a hole in you, even from this range.'

Keller sucked in a deep breath. Behind him, he heard the gambler moving forward, knew that even with the gun in his left hand, Edmonton couldn't possibly miss.

To the man in front of him, he muttered thickly, 'Do as he says, Herb.'

The tall man hesitated for a moment, then dropped the rifle, unbuckled his gunbelt and let it fall to the ground beside it.

'Now you, Keller, shuck that gun you've got in your belt.'

'Just what do you figure on doin'?' Keller rasped. 'There's more than enough gold here for all of us. You'll never get past my men out there – and don't forget Darby. He's waitin' for you somewhere close by, make no mistake about that.'

'I'll take care of him when the time comes,' Edmonton said viciously. 'You think I'm a fool? You've had it in mind to kill me since we left Twin Springs. You've just been bidin' your time until I led you here.'

Keller lowered his right hand towards his gun. While the gambler had been talking, he had listened carefully, taking in every little sound. Now he knew exactly where the other man was, about five feet directly behind him.

'All right, Edmonton, what do we do now?'

There was a pause, then Edmonton said thinly, 'Drop that gun like I said and then the two o' you are goin' to walk out o' here. You're goin' to call your men over here, tell them to drop their guns, or you'll get a bullet in the back. Otherwise—'

Before Edmonton could finish speaking, Keller took his chance, knowing it was the only one he would get if he wanted to stay alive. Swiftly, he threw himself sideways and down, pulling his Colt as he hit the ground. In almost the same instant, Edmonton pulled the trigger.

The bullet took the tall gunman in the chest, knocking him back against the rocks. Rolling swiftly, Keller saw Edmonton swinging sharply, taken off balance. He was trying to bring the derringer to bear when the heavy slug from Keller's Colt took him full in the chest.

For a moment, he stood there, swaying back on his feet, an expression of stunned shock and surprise on his thin, angular features. The small pistol fell from his nerveless fingers as his legs buckled beneath him, pitching him onto his face beside Keller's hired gunman.

With an effort, Keller pulled himself upright and stood staring down at the gambler, a mirthless grin on his face. Pain lanced through his shoulder where he had hit the ground hard. Gritting his teeth, he lurched unsteadily towards the entrance.

Alerted by the racketing gunfire, the rest of his men were already running towards the mine.

'What happened here, boss?' Clint Drexler asked, staring down at the two bodies.

'Edmonton figured he wanted all o' this gold for himself. He tried to shoot me in the back. Instead, he got Herb.'

'Leastways we don't have to share any of it with him,' Drexler muttered. He uttered a harsh laugh.

'And it was good of him to lead us to it.'

Keller bent and felt inside Edmonton's pockets. He brought out the new deeds. 'He won't be needin' these any more,' he said viciously. Turning to the men, he said, 'You'd better spread out among the rocks on either side of the entrance. We still have Darby and the other two to take care of. And remember, all of you, I want the girl alive, unharmed.'

'And Darby and the old man?'

'Those two, I want dead. That *hombre* Darby has been in my hair long enough. It's time we finished him for good.' Keller's teeth showed in a snarling grin. 'But don't make any mistakes with Darby. He's lightning fast with a gun.'

'He's only one man,' muttered one of the other gunmen. 'And that old-timer won't be too difficult to take out.'

Drexler threw a quick glance at the two bodies. 'What about these two, boss?'

'We'll have to leave 'em here for the moment. Once I'm sure there'll be no more trouble, we'll bury Herb. As for Edmonton, we'll leave him out for the vultures.'

Crouching down among the rocks, Clem checked the Winchester and then threw a quick glance towards the open mouth of the mine workings. He knew that Saunders and his companions were spread out on either side of him, ready once he gave the word.

Amy they had left much further back, out of range of any gunfire, despite her protests that she could handle a rifle as well as any of them. Hutton lay prone behind a high boulder a couple of yards away.

They had seen something of what had happened just inside the narrow tunnel and now they knew they faced only Keller and his men. Edmonton's body was just visible in the shadowed interior with that of one of Keller's men lying beside it.

Now they knew there were six men among the rocks facing them, three on either side of the mine entrance. Keller himself had gone deeper into the workings and was visible only intermittently by the light of the lamp he carried. Evidently, now that the gambler was dead, he was quite sure of himself, believing there were only two of his enemies to account for.

Out of the corner of his mouth, Colly muttered, 'It ain't goin' to be easy, prising them loose outa there, Clem.'

Nodding, Clem narrowed down his eyes. The rocks were silent mounds of shadow now and he knew Keller's men could be anywhere, but wherever they were, they had a clear shot at anyone trying to cross the stretch of open ground facing the mine. It would clearly be suicidal to attempt a frontal attack.

They had, however, one big advantage: Keller knew nothing of the four men riding with them; men who had learned the art of warfare the hard way. The plantation owner would know that Amy would take no part in any gunfight and doubtless he was reckoning on his men being able to take care of just the two of them.

Making up his mind, he said tersely, 'I reckon our

only chance is to wait for nightfall. They won't be goin' anywhere.'

He noticed the look of barely controlled anger and frustration on the old man's face, knew what was in the other's mind.

'Hellfire, Clem. We didn't come here just to sit around for hours.'

'Maybe not. But if we try it now, we'll all be shot down before we cover half o' that distance. Right now, they don't know how far we are behind 'em and pretty soon, they may start wonderin' what's happened to those other two back in the hills.'

'All right, I'll go along with you.' Colly wiped the back of his hand across his forehead.

'Good. Pass the word along to Iliff and Meredith. I'll tell Saunders and Cordell.'

He waited until the old man had moved silently away into the rocks and then worked his way through the maze of boulders, keeping his head well down. He found the two men crouched in a hollow thirty yards away, saw them jerk their head round at his approach, then relax.

'We've got no chance of takin' them in daylight,' he said softly. 'We'll have to wait for nightfall. Then we move in from both sides.'

Both men nodded in agreement. 'Just like the old days, Lieutenant,' Saunders said. 'What do we do if they reckon we're still miles away, or taken out by those two back there, and decide to come out to take a look?'

Clem's face was a mask of grim determination as he replied, 'If that should happen, we'll let them

151

have all we've got. Somehow, I figure Keller's ain't goin' anywhere. He'll wait to hear from his lookouts before he does anythin'.'

'Makes sense, I guess.' Cordell gave a brief nod. 'We'll wait for your word.' He lifted his head slightly and threw a quick glance at the sky. 'It looks as though this overcast is goin' to stay for a while. There won't be any moon tonight. That should give us an edge.'

'Let's hope so,' Clem replied. 'Even in the dark, it ain't going to be easy.'

Going back to his former position, he stretched himself out in as comfortable position as possible. A couple of minutes later, Colly came wriggling back. 'I gave 'em your message,' he said, in low tones. 'They both know what to do.'

'Good. Now all we can do it wait.'

It was a long, slow wait. At any moment, they expected a shot to come from the rocks on the far side of the depression, but the intense silence held. The only movement visible was that of Keller, occasionally showing as a dark silhouette as he prowled around the inside of the tunnel, his progress marked out by the shifting glow of the lamp.

At irregular intervals, he would make his way outside, standing a few feet from the entrance, switching his glance from one side to the other. As time went on, the intervals between his appearances just inside the tunnel became progressively shorter. It was clear to Clem that he was becoming more and more worried and nervous.

By now, it must have occurred to him that something had gone wrong with his plans. Clem had the feeling that he had expected word from one or both of the men he had posted along the trail, informing him that there was no longer any danger from the men following him.

At that moment, Keller would be hoping that he and Colly were dead and Amy had been captured. Clearly, the lack of any news was grating on the other man's nerves.

With the thick, lowering clouds still covering the sky, darkness fell quickly. Giving the signal to Colly to alert Meredith and Iliff, he slid to his left, finding the other two men where he had left them.

'We'll hit them now,' he said tightly. 'You reckon the two o' you can make it across there and take 'em from that side? Saunders and Cordell are goin' in the other way. Colly and me will hit 'em from the front.'

It was impossible to make out the expressions on the men's faces, but he saw them both give a quick nod. 'Good. Give me a couple o' minutes to get into position.'

'You can rely on us, Lieutenant,' Cordell said.

Moving back, Clem studied the rocks and ledges for a long moment, searching for any sign of movement. There was nothing. Wherever those six men were concealed, they were giving nothing away.

Lifting the rifle, he aimed swiftly at the only thing he could see – Ed Keller, still deep inside the tunnel. He saw him jerk sideways, then go down onto his knees and crawl swiftly towards the rock wall, extinguishing the lamp at the same time. Clearly, his shot had missed.

The next moment, gunfire erupted from the rocks facing them. Leaving the rifle, he tugged the Colts from their holsters and moved swiftly down the steep drop, occasionally sliding on his back. Slugs ricocheted off the boulders all around him.

In a minor avalanche of rocks and stones, Colly came down behind him. At the bottom, Clem made a dash across the thirty yards of open ground, weaving from side to side. To both his left and right, there was the racketing thunder of more gunfire as Saunders and the others swung around from both sides.

Bullets pecked at the ground beside him but a half minute later, he was crouched against the rocks to the left of the tunnel entrance. Sucking in deep breaths, he pushed himself hard against the stone, peering up into the blackness. A stab of gunflame appeared almost directly above him.

Jerking up the Colts, he loosed off a couple of shots. Neither of the slugs ricocheted and a second later, he picked out a low, moaning grunt and knew that both had gone home.

A couple of feet away, Colly was a dark shadow, his back pressed hard against a large boulder. His rifle barked twice before he threw himself back as return fire hammered against the boulder. More lead hummed around Clem as he struggled to make out where the rest of Keller's men were.

He knew Keller had split his force with three men on either side of the tunnel. One was either dead or badly wounded just above him, his body probably jammed into the rocks. Swiftly, he turned his head to look back along the steep hillside. The gunfire in that direction had now risen to a crescendo and he guessed that Saunders and Cordell were working their way up onto the ledges.

A sudden, high-pitched yell broke through the racket and in the dimness, he saw a limp body fall some twenty feet before hitting the ground. A moment later, there came a sudden, unexpected lull in the firing.

Swiftly, Clem rammed more shells into the empty chambers of his Colts. A moment later, a harsh voice called, 'Hold your fire, we're comin' down.'

Alert for a trick, Clem yelled back, 'Toss your guns down. Then come down with your hands lifted where we can see 'em.'

From somewhere inside the tunnel, Keller yelled, 'Keep firing! There's six o' you and only two o' them.'

Another voice rang out, 'You're wrong, Mr Keller. There's a whole bunch of 'em. They've already killed four of us. We don't stand a chance.'

There was a long silence, then Clem called, 'You'd better believe him, Keller. There are more of us out here than you bargained for. This is the end as far as you're concerned. Better come out and give yourself up – or we'll come in and get you.'

A clatter among the rocks told him that the remaining men had tossed their guns away. A minute later, two figures edged their way down the boulder-strewn side, then came forward with their hands raised.

Sharply, Clem said, 'Keep your rifle on 'em, Colly.

The first wrong move they make, shoot 'em.'

'You can be sure o' that,' Colly grated.

Less than five minutes later, Saunders and his three companions emerged from the darkness. There was a dark stain on Cordell's left sleeve which Clem noticed instantly.

Glancing down at it, the other man said quietly, 'Nothin' but a flesh wound, Clem.' A pause, then he added, 'Where's Keller?'

Clem jerked his Colt in the direction of the dark opening. 'Still in there. I guess we'll have to flush him out.' He turned to where Colly still had his rifle trained on the two gunhawks. 'How far in does that tunnel go?' he asked.

'Not far. About twenty-five yards, I reckon.'

'No other way out? No side tunnels?'

Colly shook his head. He made to say something more, then swung sharply at a movement in the distance. Amy came running toward them. She stopped uncertainly as Clem waved her back while she was still several yards away.

'I heard the shooting stop and came to see what was happening,' she said.

'Stay where you are,' Clem told her. 'We've got Keller holed up in there and he's armed.'

A few feet away, Hutton said tautly, 'I'll go in and get that polecat. I know the place better than anyone and after what he was goin' to do with my grand-daughter, I—'

'You'll stay right where you are, old-timer,' Clem said sharply. 'He's mine. I told him once before that the next time I met him, I'd kill him.'

156

Before Colly could protest further, Clem moved quickly towards the tunnel entrance, edging slowly along the rocks. Hefting the Colt in his right hand, he waited for a moment, then flung himself swiftly around the side, dropping to his knees as he did so.

The shot from the interior came almost at once. It struck the wall within an inch of his head and ricocheted off with a thin whine. Swiftly, he fired at the spot where the gunflame had come from, but Keller had already moved away, deeper into the dense blackness.

In the utter silence, Clem strained to pick out the slightest sound which would give the other man way. Now, he knew, it was a question of whose nerve would hold out the longest. He guessed Keller was a hardened killer. A man didn't get to the position he had in New Orleans without ruthlessly killing anyone who stood in his way.

The silence lengthened, drew down on him from all sides. He had no idea how many rounds the other had on him for that Colt he carried, but—

He stiffened. A faint sound reached him out of the enveloping darkness. It was the sigh a man made when he had been holding his breath too long and had been forced to let it out.

Aiming swiftly, he squeezed the trigger twice. In the brief flashes of gunflame, he had fragmentary glimpses of Keller standing against the rock wall less than ten feet away. The Colt was in his hand but he seemed unable to lift it.

In the ensuing darkness, he distinctly heard the scrape of boots on the rough floor as Keller slid down the wall. Slowly, Clem's eyes adjusted to the darkness. He could just make out the body slumped against the stone, the legs thrust out to their full length.

Going forward cautiously, he pushed Keller's shoulder with his foot, his finger still hard on the trigger. But there was no need for a further shot. Keller fell limply sideways and lay still.

Sucking air into his lungs, Clem went back to where the others were waiting. 'It's over,' he said simply. 'Keller's dead. I guess his greed got the better of him.'

'What do we do with these two?' Colly asked, indicating the two gunmen.

Clem's features were grim as he faced the men standing sullenly a few feet from the mine entrance. 'Reckon we've got two choices,' he said evenly. 'There ain't no law in Devil's Reach so we either try 'em ourselves, find 'em guilty, and hang 'em – or they fork their mounts, ride out o' here, and keep goin'.'

He knew from the looks on the men's faces what their choice would be. Finally, after a long pause, he said, 'Get out o' here and don't come back or we'll be waitin' for you.'

Without looking back, the men stumbled off into the darkness to where they had left their horses. A few minutes later, they picked out the sound of hoofbeats in the distance.

'Guess we'll be ridin' out soon,' Saunders said soberly. 'We—'

'Not a chance,' Colly broke in vehemently. 'I need

you men here to help me get that gold out. After all that's happened, there'll be an equal six-way share. It'll take us around six months, but we can find some place to stay in those shacks yonder.'

He glanced round at Clem where he stood close beside Amy. 'I know that when we first met, you were headed all the way west to California. But I reckon that can wait for six months. With your share, you can do a hell of a lot once you get there.'

Glancing down at Amy, Clem said quietly, 'You know, Colly, right now, I want somethin' that's worth more than all the gold you've got in there.'

He saw Colly give a knowing nod and when he looked back at Amy, he guessed from the look in her eyes, she knew exactly what he meant.